Deborah Raney

Raney Day Press

***Playing for Keeps***

*Playing by Heart,* a Carol Award winner and Christy Award finalist, was originally published in 2004. In 2014 the story was revised and published as *A January Bride*, part of the *Winter Brides* collection. Now, two decades later in 2024, Raney Day Press is delighted to offer *Playing for Keeps*, the all new sequel, collected with *Playing by Heart* in this two-novella volume.



Published by Raney Day Press

Cover design by Ken Raney

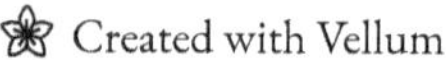 Created with Vellum

*Playing for Keeps* is the brand-new sequel to *Playing by Heart*.
This new collection contains both of these charming novellas in one volume.

In ***Playing by Heart***, young English professor Arthur Tyler struggles to manage the bed and breakfast he and his wife, Annie, owned before her untimely death. Lonely, he jumps at the chance to offer temporary office space at the inn for the new neighbor of his elderly friend Ginny. It turns out Madeleine Houser is a successful author whose novels Annie had read voraciously. Since Art is always teaching when Maddie is writing at the inn, they've never met, but learn to know each other through daily notes and text messages. A major misunderstanding takes a decidedly romantic turn when Art and Maddie finally meet and discover each other's true identity. Even so, there are obstacles to overcome before their romance can blossom.

The love story of Art and Maddie continues in ***Playing for Keeps***. But their fledgling marriage faces challenges when expectations collide. Now, newlyweds Art and Maddie are struggling to find their way together. When Maddie is offered a chance to take a research trip to Paris, it appears a short separation might help them both figure out what happily-ever-after looks like for them. Yet even the beautiful City of Lights is lonely without the man she loves with all her heart, and with five thousand miles separating them, how can they ever work things out when different time zones and frenzied schedules conspire to keep them incommunicado?

***Playing by Heart***, a Carol Award winner and Christy Award finalist, was originally published in 2004. In 2014 the story was revised and published as *A January Bride*, part of the *Winter Brides* collection. Now, two decades later in 2024, Raney Day Press is delighted to offer *Playing for Keeps,* the all new sequel to *Playing by Heart*, both collected in this two-novella volume.

*For Ken, love of my life*

Deborah Raney

One

Surveying the chaos around her, Madeleine Houser set her coffee mug on the dining room table and shoved another packing carton out of her path. It didn't budge. She bent over and attempted to read the smudged label. *Kitchen—good china*. Oh. Good thing she'd resisted the temptation to kick the box.

Maddie looked into the kitchen where cupboards gaped open, hinges naked. The cabinet doors were lined up against the wall in the empty breakfast nook. Even after four days, the smell of wet enamel stung her nostrils. The flooring couldn't be laid until the electrician fixed the mess he'd made of the wiring. And she didn't dare put her china in the cupboards until all that was finished.

What had her sister gotten her into? Kate's husband had been transferred to Ohio, but with their mother in the nursing home here in Clayburn, Kate had begged her to leave her beloved New York loft and move into Kate and Jed's house on Harper Street while it was being refurbished to sell. "You can write anywhere, Maddie," Kate had pled in her best big-sister voice. "Besides, you can sublet the loft, and just think what you'll save on the rent."

So here she was in Clayburn, Kansas—the middle of nowhere —proving quite soundly that one could not write just *anywhere*.

Lugging the carton of china out of the way, she wove her way through the maze of boxes and poured another cup of coffee. She blew a long strand of dishwater-blond hair out of her eyes and slid into a dining room chair. In the midst of the piles of books and boxes and unsorted mail strewn across the table, her laptop computer glared accusingly at her.

Ignoring the disorder, she pulled the computer close, pushed her glasses up on her nose, and tried to remember where she'd left off. Ah yes. The heartless landlord had just evicted the young widow. *Oh brother, Houser, how cliché can you get?* Well, too bad. She didn't have time to change the whole plot now. She'd managed to write nearly two thousand words this morning, but given her track record lately, she'd be lucky if fifty of them were worth keeping.

What had she been thinking to let her editor to talk her into a January 1 deadline in the midst of this cross-country move? It was nearly October! "You can do it, Madeleine," Janice had crooned in her conniving editor's voice. "If we can get this book on the shelves before next Christmas, the first print run will sell out in a month. Come on. Say you'll do it. Houser fans are clamoring for your next book."

Over the six years Janice Hudson had been Maddie's editor, they'd become dear friends. But right now Maddie wanted to strangle her.

She edited the sentence in front of the blinking cursor and forced herself to return to the nineteenth century and the plight of Anne Caraway, her suffering heroine. Poor Anne. She'd lost her beloved William, and been evicted from her home, alone with a small child to care for. Now, Maddie was about to throw Anne Caraway onto the mean streets of Chicago. It was the bane of an author's existence—this need to make her beloved characters suffer. To put them in the furnace and turn up the fire. But without conflict, there was no story, and conflict often equaled sorrow. So onto the streets Anne Caraway and little Charlie must go. She typed furiously.

The faint echo of dripping water pierced her concentration. She glanced up from her laptop and tilted her head, listening. Was it raining? Who could tell with the heavy drapes covering the room's high windows? Those would have to go. But first she must finish this book. Brushing off the temptation to get up and check outside, she turned back to the keyboard. She typed twenty words before the *drip, drip, drip* became demanding.

She pushed her chair back and navigated the labyrinth of cardboard boxes. The sound seemed to be coming from the kitchen, but nothing was leaking there as far as she could tell. Dodging sawhorses the contractors had left, she crossed to the basement door. As a rule, basements gave her the creeps, but in this tornado alley on the Kansas prairie, it was a rare house that didn't have one. She'd been relieved to find Kate and Jed's charming Tudor had only a closet-sized cellar. Just enough space to provide refuge from a cyclone, but not enough to have dank corners where. . .well, where whatever it was she was afraid of could hide.

She opened the door––and gasped. The wooden treads at the bottom of the flight glistened with moisture, and from the far end of the cellar, she could hear the unmistakable sound of water trickling into more water. A naked lightbulb hung over the stairs. *Are you kidding me?* The string attached to the pull chain was caught on one of the splintered rafters overhead. Maddie straddled the steps, one foot on the top landing, the other on the thin ledge that ran the length of the stairwell. Grabbing the door handle for support, she scooted along the ledge, grasping blindly for the string.

Next thing she knew, she was teetering on the ledge. She reached for something to steady herself. Unfortunately, what she found was the door, which slammed shut behind her.

The stairwell went dark. Miraculously she found the string with the next random swing of her arm. Not so miraculously when she pulled on the chain, the light flickered, then sparked.

She heard the ominous sound of every electronic device in the house powering down.

Had she remembered to save her manuscript? The old laptop barely held a charge any more; it would be dead before the auto-save kicked in. She felt herself slipping and gasped when she hit the stairs. Hard. A sharp pain sliced through her left ankle, and she bumped down half the flight of stairs.

When the stairwell quit spinning she crawled back up to the kitchen and pulled herself to her feet, testing. *Ouch!* Her ankle had already swollen to the size of a small grapefruit. Damp and aching, she hobbled to a chair and sank into it. Her cell phone was upstairs in the guest room charging. Now what? Rubbing her ankle, she remembered that Kate still had a landline phone in the dining room. Thankfully, there was a dial tone. She rummaged through the desk drawer until she found the list her sister had left with the phone number of her neighbor, Ginny Ross. Ginny answered on the second ring.

"Ginny? Hi, it's Madeleine Houser next door. Is your electricity out?"

"No. Well, at least I don't believe so. Just a minute. . ."

Maddie heard an oven door creak open and then what sounded like the ding of a microwave. "No. Everything's still on over here."

She gave a low growl. "I think I've blown another fuse. And there's water in the—ouch!"

"Madeleine? What's happened? Are you all right?"

Maddie cringed as she eased into the desk chair. "I'm fine. I fell down the stairs and sprained my ankle."

"You scared me. I thought you'd electrocuted yourself."

Maddie gave a humorless laugh. "Nothing so dramatic, I'm afraid. Sorry to bother you. I just didn't want to call the electrician again if it was only—"

"I'll be right over."

The phone went dead, and Maddie sat staring at the receiver for a few seconds, until she realized Ginny meant her words literally. Maddie had met her neighbor only two weeks ago, but already she'd grown to love the woman. At eighty-four and widowed for a quarter of a century, Ginny epitomized the word *spry*. She was as independent as any of Maddie's thirty-something New York friends. With her own mother's mind ravaged by Alzheimer's disease, it was good to have a wise older woman to talk to.

"Yoo-hoo!" Ginny's cheery voice floated in from the mudroom.

"Come on in, Ginny. But watch your step."

Ginny bustled into the kitchen, weaving her way through sawhorses and stepladders. "Now what did you do to yourself?" She bent to inspect Maddie's swollen ankle. "Oh my! Are you sure it's not broken?"

"I don't think so." She rubbed the tender area around the swelling.

Ginny scooted another chair close and helped Maddie elevate her foot. Then she went to the freezer and rummaged inside until she unearthed a package of frozen peas. "Here we go." She wrapped the icy bag in a dishcloth and draped it over Maddie's ankle. She glanced around the kitchen, taking in the renovation chaos. "How are you ever going to finish that book in this mess?"

Maddie couldn't help it. Tears that had been pent up for weeks overflowed. "Oh, Ginny, I'm already so far behind I can't imagine how I'll make my deadline. And without electricity, I'm sunk."

"Well, of course you are." Ginny made sympathetic clucking noises with her tongue and surveyed the kitchen again. "This will never do. I'd offer to let you write at my house, but I'm afraid my beginning piano students would make this wreck seem like a haven of peace."

Maddie swiped at a tear and forced a smile. "I appreciate that, Ginny. But it's not your problem. I'll figure something out. Maybe I can just go to the library. . . ."

"Are you kidding? You'd have a constant stream of onlookers

gawking and pestering you with questions." Ginny snapped her fingers and turned to Maddie with a triumphant gleam in her eyes. "I know just the place. My friend Arthur Tyler has that monstrous house sitting empty ever since his Annabeth died. They had a booming bed-and-breakfast until Annabeth got so bad. Arthur rarely has guests at the inn now, so I know he wouldn't mind if you went there to write. You probably wouldn't want to stay overnight, but you could use one of the rooms for an office. Arthur is a professor at the university. Keeps saying he's going to retire, but he never does."

Maddie hesitated. "Where is this place, Ginny?" She felt awkward about the whole idea, but she had to do something. She sure wasn't going to get her book finished here.

"It's just a couple miles east of town. Out on Hampton Road. Pretty little place. Peaceful. Annabeth's parents ran the inn for years. Named it after her, of course. Grover and I stayed there for our fortieth anniversary. Seemed kind of silly to stay overnight two miles from home, but it was nice. Kind of romantic. . ." A faraway look came to Ginny's eyes, and an ever-so-faint blush touched her powdered cheeks. "Let me give Arthur a call. You just get the plumber and electrician here. I'll take care of everything else."

*Two*

Maddie stood in the doorway of the inn and inhaled. Sunlight splashed saffron patches on the shiny wood floors and caused the jewel tones in the window coverings and upholstery to glow. In spite of her injured ankle, she felt better already, standing in the spacious parlor and looking into tidy rooms free of packing crates.

"Arthur said to make yourself at home." Ginny dropped a key ring into the pocket of her bulky sweater and ran a hand over the oak mantle. Her fingertips left a trail in the film of dust. She cluck-clucked and shook her gray head. "Annabeth always kept this place spotless. Even after she got so sick. Poor Arthur. . ."

"Was Annabeth a friend of yours?"

"She was. A dear friend. She and Arthur both. It was a terrible thing, her dying." Ginny lifted a heavy pewter candlestick and wiped the dust away with the sleeve of her sweater.

"I'm so sorry. . . ."

Ginny nodded, then gave a resolute bob of her chin and brightened. "I'd show you the rest of the house, but I don't think your ankle would appreciate that steep staircase yet. Arthur said you could set up shop in one of the guest rooms. He lives in the apartment on the lower level—doesn't use any of the house proper—so I'm sure you'd be welcome to use the main living area here if you prefer. Or you could hole up in this bedroom." Ginny opened the wide French doors off the living room to reveal a guest room beautifully decorated with dark, Old English antiques. "It's the only guest room on the main floor. And by the way, the only bathroom on the first floor is in here."

Maddie poked her head into the room and took in the modern pedestal sink on the far wall just outside a door that apparently concealed the bath.

Ginny pulled the doors closed and led the way through a wide arched doorway into the dining room. To the left, an open staircase led down to the apartment where the proprietor lived, Maddie presumed. The steep stairway was defended by an oak railing, and in the middle of the dining room sat a huge, round, antique oak table on an oriental rug. The walls wore old-fashioned wallpaper in shades of plum and burnished gold. A fine antique buffet held a silver tea service and baskets of teas and jams. Beyond that, an open doorway led to a small galley kitchen, where an array of dishes and baskets and jars of canned goods were displayed on open shelving.

"You're sure Mr. Tyler won't care if I set up right here?" Maddie tipped her head toward the dining-room table.

"I'd say this is perfect," Ginny said, obviously pleased with herself. "I'll leave now so you can get to work."

"Oh, Ginny, it *is* perfect. How can I ever thank you?"

Ginny winked. "Just finish that book, sweetie. I've only about three chapters before I finish my last Houser novel, and then I'm fresh out of reading material."

Ginny bustled out the front door, and Maddie was left in the blessed quiet of the old house. She took her laptop from its case and set it on the table, positioning her chair for a lovely view through the arched doorway all the way to the front hall. She connected the power adaptor and plugged it in. When she was satisfied with the arrangement, she unpacked her sack lunch and hobbled into the kitchen to put it away.

The refrigerator shelves were empty save for a few cans of soda and a package of ground coffee. Maddie put her lunch on the middle shelf, feeling strangely as though she were trespassing. But Ginny had said Arthur Tyler insisted she have free run of the place, including full use of the little kitchen.

She dumped the dark sludge from the coffeemaker's carafe and found fresh filters in a drawer under the counter. Once the coffee was brewing, Maddie went back to the dining room to finish setting up shop. She unloaded her bag, placing her dictionary and several reference books to her left, notebook and pen to her right.

She selected several hours of Mozart sonatas on her computer. Classical music filled the room, and Maddie sighed as she sank into the brocade padded chair, slipped off her shoes, and propped her swollen ankle on the seat of a neighboring chair. The timeless melody, the rich aroma of fresh coffee, and her Victorian surroundings transported her back in time. And when she put her fingers to the keyboard, the words flowed as they hadn't in months. *I don't know you, Arthur Tyler, but God bless your generous old heart.*

For the next two hours, Maddie typed, getting up only to refill her coffee mug. Her plot was moving along nicely when a polite *meow* made her look up from her computer.

A monstrous gray-and-white cat stuck its head through the stairway balusters and peered at her. Coming up the last steps, the cat sashayed over to Maddie, arched its back, and rubbed against her ankle before plopping down on her right foot.

Maddie took off her glasses and laid them on the table. "Well, hello there, kitty." She reached down to stroke the leonine head. "They didn't tell me about you."

The cat purred in response and nestled closer to Maddie. Though the house didn't have the chill she'd expected of a high-ceilinged Victorian, the cat's warmth was welcome. The old schoolhouse clock on the wall over the stairwell ticked a reassuring cadence, and she wrote for another hour while the cat napped.

The clock's muffled chime and the growl of her own stomach brought Maddie out of Anne Caraway's world and back to the present. Wiggling her toes and lowering her left foot from its elevated position on the other chair, she nudged the cat. "Sorry, kitty, but I need to get up and stretch a bit."

The cat yawned, bowed his back, and gave a short, friendly *mew* before following her into the kitchen. Maddie took her lunch from the refrigerator and ate it, leaning against the kitchen counter, her mind still on her story. Though her ankle throbbed, it felt good to stand up and flex her muscles a bit. After she finished her sandwich, she filled the sink with warm, sudsy water and washed the dishes, putting them to drain on the old-fashioned wire dish rack. She'd forgotten how nice it was to be in an operational kitchen, and she spent a few extra minutes tidying the kitchen before she went back to her computer.

Her feline friend had disappeared. The clock chimed the half hour and she looked up, surprised to find it was two thirty already. Checking her word count, she was thrilled to discover she'd written nearly three thousand words. A few more days like this and she might actually believe she could make her deadline. She closed her laptop and began gathering her belongings.

Before she left, she scratched out a note for the inn's owner.

*Dear Mr. Tyler,*

*Thank you so much for allowing me to work from your lovely home. It was such a peaceful day, and I accomplished more than I'd hoped. I so appreciate your generosity, and if you're certain it's not too much of an inconvenience, I'll plan to come back tomorrow.*

*Madeleine Houser*

*P.S. Your cat was a wonderful companion. He kept my feet*

*toasty warm while I worked. What is his name? He is a "he," isn't he?*

The following morning, the plumber and the electrician arrived on the doorstep at eight o'clock sharp. Maddie left them instructions, then hauled her laptop and research books out to her Mazda and drove the eight blocks to the nursing home to check in on her mother before heading to the inn.

A nurse at the front desk greeted her when she came in. "You're Mildred Houser's daughter, aren't you?"

Maddie nodded. "How's she doing this morning?"

"About the same, I guess." The nurse gave her a look that spoke volumes.

With a heavy heart, Maddie trudged down the hall. Her mother was slumped in a chair in her room, staring out the window with that vacant look Maddie had come to despise. It struck her that at sixty-eight, her mother looked older and far more frail than Ginny Ross did at eighty-four.

She took a thin hand in hers. "Good morning, Mom."

No response.

"Your hands are cold. Do you want your sweater?"

Without looking at Maddie, her mother stretched out her arm and with birdlike motions brushed at something invisible on the windowsill.

"It's a beautiful day, Mom. September's almost over. Maybe we can go for a walk when I come back this evening."

She might as well have talked to the wall. Sighing, she went to the closet and picked out a lightweight sweater. As she started to close the sliding door, she noticed something leaning against a far corner of the closet—several old canes she and Kate had bought for their mother when Mom first started losing her balance. On impulse, Maddie chose one of the canes and tested it. It did ease the pressure on her ankle. "I'm going to borrow this for a couple days, Mom, okay?"

No reply. She closed the closet door and went to drape the sweater over her mother's shoulders. She patted Mom's frail hand. "I need to run, but I'll check in on you before dinner tonight, okay?"

Her mother turned slowly from the window and looked from the cane to Maddie's face. For one brief moment, Maddie thought she saw a spark of recognition in the rheumy eyes. But as quickly as it had come, it was gone, and Maddie was left with a familiar dull ache in her heart. *Oh, Mom. I miss you so much.*

Maddie arrived at the inn before nine o'clock. She hadn't noticed before what a beautiful setting the charming house occupied. With a shelter belt of Osage orange trees to the east and a stand of cottonwoods far to the south, the three-story house stood sentinel on the Kansas plains. A late September cool spell had left the trees and shrubs tinged with a hint of the autumn-to-come, but pink- and peach-colored roses were still in bloom, climbing the trellis by the front porch.

Maddie got out of her car and breathed in the country air. Attempting to use her mother's cane, she slung her computer bag and purse over one shoulder and tucked the sack lunch she'd brought under her arm. She hobbled up the steps to the wide wraparound porch, found the key in the mailbox beside the door, and let herself in.

On the dining room table was a message penned in a tidy masculine script on the back of the note she'd written the day before.

*Dear Ms. Houser,*

*I'm delighted you enjoyed the time you spent here yesterday. I apologize for the dust and cobwebs. The inn has been a bit neglected since my wife's death. But I'm glad you were able to make use of it. Please do continue to come for as long as you like.*

*And thank you for washing up the dishes. I'm sorry to have left the kitchen in such a mess. I rarely have guests at the inn during the week, but I did have someone drop in Tuesday night and didn't get a chance to clean up before I left to teach my eight o'clock class. I shall try to do better in the future.*

*Arthur Tyler*

*P.S. The cat's name is Alex. And yes, "he" is a he. I hope he hasn't been a pest. As you probably discovered, he has no claws so is banned from the great outdoors, but please feel free to shoo him downstairs if he becomes obnoxious. Ginny tells me you have a horrendous deadline, and I'd hate to be responsible—even by proxy —for you not meeting it. (And I confess I haven't read any of your writing yet, but if Ginny has her way, that shall be remedied very quickly.)*

Tucking the note into her computer bag, Maddie smiled. What a charming old gentleman Ginny's friend was! Ginny had said Arthur Tyler was looking to retire but still taught English at one of the colleges in Wichita. She wondered if his lengthy missive was due to the English professor in him or merely to loneliness. A little of both, she suspected.

She set up her laptop and started a pot of coffee. While it brewed, she tidied up the kitchen, taking care to put the vintage canisters and a pretty Franciscan Apple teapot back in their original spots after she wiped the dusty countertop underneath them. She found a dust cloth and furniture polish under the sink and polished the dining room table and buffet. She hated cleaning her own house, but it was different here. Besides, it was the least she could do if the proprietor wouldn't let her pay for the time she was spending here.

When the luscious aroma of Irish cream café reached her nostrils, Maddie filled a large mug and placed it beside her laptop. But before she opened the file that contained her novel, she penned another note to Mr. Tyler.

*Dear Mr. Tyler,*

*Alex is not a pest at all! I've thoroughly enjoyed his company. I had a cat once myself, when I was a little girl. But since I began writing, I haven't had time to take care of one.*

*Please don't think another minute about the "dust and cobwebs." I didn't even notice.*

She read the last line again. Not exactly the truth. She scratched out a word and changed the sentence to read: *I barely even noticed.* She signed the note, then put her fingers on the keyboard and delved happily into Anne Caraway's world.

*Three*

Arthur Tyler pulled into the driveway with a weary sigh. The cheerful-looking sign in front of the house read, "Welcome to Annabeth's Inn," but it would never again feel like a welcoming place to him. Not without his Annie.

If this was what thirty-nine felt like, Art couldn't imagine living to be as old as his friend Ginny. Ginny Ross had been Annie's friend first, but as the cancer had sucked away Annabeth's young life, the older woman had taken Art under her wing. As if she and Annie were co-conspirators, Ginny's friendship had gradually been transferred to him. It was Annie's last gift to him, and he was grateful.

Annie had been gone for two and a half years now. Sometimes it seemed forever, and Art struggled to remember how the music of her voice had sounded, how her skin had felt beneath his touch. Other times it seemed as though she would come bounding down the stairs any minute, wearing her pixie smile and the shimmer in her eyes that spoke of how much she loved him.

He parked outside the garage, slammed the door of his pickup, and walked back down the drive to the mailbox. The first day of October had blown in on a chill wind, and he turned up the collar of his overcoat. He pulled down the arched door of the mailbox. Junk. A couple of Christmas catalogs, and the gas bill, which would be outrageously high—even higher next month, now that he was leaving the heat on during the day for Ginny's writer friend. But what did he care? He had nothing else to spend his money on.

*Be still and know that I am God.* The words floated through his brain, scolding him for his attitude. "Sorry, Lord," he whispered, his footsteps crunching on the gravel drive. He walked around the house and turned the key in the side door that led to his basement apartment. He stepped into the empty foyer. A *thump, thump, thump* on the steps brought a slight smile to his face. Alex. Another gift from Annie. He'd hated cats—or thought he did—until Annie had coaxed this mangy stray off the highway and into his heart. Now Alex greeted him with a comical cross between a purr and a meow, arched his back, and rubbed up tight against Art's pant leg.

Art stooped to scratch the cat under his chin. "Hey, Alex. What's for supper?" He put the mail on the bar in the kitchenette and hung up his coat in the bedroom closet. Alex trotted after him as he climbed the stairs to the inn to make sure Ginny's friend hadn't left the door unlocked or the coffeemaker on. He was glad the woman was able to use the house as a getaway. It would have made Annie happy to think of having a real author staying in the house—*writing* here. Annie had read all of Madeleine Houser's books. Ginny had seen to that, giving her the most recent release each year for Christmas.

He'd never paid much attention to them, leaning as he did toward the classics. He taught Tolstoy, Dostoevsky, Dickens, and Jane Austen at the university. With passion. And he'd always teased Annie about the fluffy romance novels she read. He assumed that was what Madeleine Houser wrote, though it was beyond him how someone Ginny's age could even remember what romance was. A wry smile touched his lips. *Who are you to talk, Tyler? Do you remember?*

Oh, but he did. That was the problem. He brushed away the memories as if they were cobwebs.

As he came up the steps to the inn's dining room, his gaze landed on something under the table. He went to investigate and found a smooth wooden cane with an ornately carved handle. Apparently the author had dropped it and been unable to reach it beneath the table. Funny she hadn't mentioned it. He pictured the doddering woman trying to navigate his porch steps without her cane and shuddered. The last thing he needed was a lawsuit. But glancing around the room, he noticed the furniture gleamed in the afternoon sun. Madeleine Houser's dust rag had struck again. The woman had come to the inn four weekdays in a row now, and each day he came home to a tidier house than the day before. She must not be *too* infirm.

On the table, he spied a sheet of stationery filled with handwriting that was now familiar. They'd gotten in the habit of writing little notes back and forth concerning the details of their arrangement. Art had rather enjoyed their brief correspondence. Ha! What did it say about him that he received such pleasure exchanging notes with an old woman he'd never set eyes on?

He picked up her note and read.

*Dear Mr. Tyler,*

*Once again, thank you for opening your home to me. The plumber finally got the water problems solved, but the electrical work is taking longer than expected and the man who was to lay the flooring called this morning to say he's a week behind schedule with his other jobs. I'm so sorry. I certainly don't mean to burden you with my problems. I only mention them to explain why I continue to take advantage of your kind offer. Please, if this becomes a burden for you, I hope you'll say something. I could easily go to the library to write if this is not working out for you.*

*Also, I don't mean to pry, but I noticed Alex seemed a bit listless this morning. I wondered if you'd noticed? I didn't see him at all this afternoon. I hope he's okay. I've grown quite fond of my little foot-warmer.*

*Thank you again,*
*Madeleine Houser*

Arthur set the note down and stooped to pick up Alex. "Are you feeling okay, Buddy?" The cat looked perfectly healthy purring away in his arms. Art gave the furry chin a good scratching. "Maybe Ms. Houser just doesn't realize how old you're getting to be."

He put Alex on the floor and sat down at the table to reply to the note. Turning over Madeleine Houser's stationery, he wrote on the back:

*Dear Ms. Houser,*

*First of all, please do not apologize again. I am delighted to have you here, especially as it seems that every evening when I come home, one less dirty dish sits in the sink and one more piece of furniture is free of dust. Housekeeping services were certainly not part of the agreement we made, but I confess I don't want to complain too loudly. In all seriousness, I appreciate the tidying up you've done more than you can know.*

*Second, please call me Art. I hear Mr. Tyler a hundred times a day from my students, and though you and I have never met, I'd like to think we could be on a first-name basis by now.*

*Third matter of business: As you've probably discovered, you forgot your cane here today. I found it under the table. I've left it for you in the kitchen. Hope you haven't missed it too much.*

*And finally: As for Alex, I'll keep an eye on him, but I haven't noticed anything out of the ordinary. He's a bit of a couch potato, and like the rest of us, I suppose, he is getting along in years. But thank you for your concern. I'll tell him you asked after him.*


He smiled at his little joke, scrawled a happy face beside it, and signed his name. He hoped the old woman was getting as much enjoyment from their note swapping as he was. His step a bit lighter, he went down to his apartment to fix a sandwich and grade the essays his advanced English students had turned in.

Four

By the end of the following week, Maddie had settled into a comfortable routine. She consulted with the workmen before leaving the house, made a quick visit to the nursing home, and usually reached her makeshift desk in the inn's dining room by nine A.M.

On Friday morning, Maddie let the electrician in and headed out, loaded down with packages to mail. Miracle of miracles, she had ten more chapters of her manuscript ready to ship off to Peggy Barton, the woman who proofread her first drafts. Her editors didn't expect her to turn in a perfect manuscript, but Maddie cringed at the thought of her professional editors seeing her rough first draft. She'd always hired someone to proof her work before she sent it off. Peggy was old-school, preferring to work from hard copies rather than a digital file, but she was good, so Maddie humored her.

Kate had asked Maddie to get some things out of storage, so she had those boxes ready to mail to her sister as well.

She parked in front of the quaint post office and went around to the passenger side for the packages. Though she still favored her left leg a bit, her ankle was much better, and she'd returned her mother's cane the day after retrieving it from the inn. Piling the parcels in her arms, she gave the car door a shove with one hip and started up the sidewalk.

As she approached the double doors of the post office building, a dark-haired man exited and held the door open for her.

"Thanks so much." She smiled at him over her tower of packages.

"No problem." The smile he flashed in return did funny things to her insides.

*Forget it, Houser,* she warned herself, catching the man's departing reflection in the glass. *He's probably married. Besides, you've given up on men, remember?*

The man greeted another patron by name, then stopped on the sidewalk outside to talk to an elderly couple. Ah, small-town life. Clayburn was possibly one of the last towns in America without home delivery, so the post office was a social hub. She liked the fact that everybody seemed to know everybody else. In her New York neighborhood, no one bothered to exchange more than polite nods.

She dropped off her packages, picked up three days' worth of mail, and drove out to Annabeth's Inn. After two weeks of writing there each day, pulling into the inn's driveway had begun to feel like home. She wasn't sure she'd be able to write in the house on Harper Street once it was livable again, and she was beginning to wish she hadn't prayed so hard for the plumber and electrician to hurry.

She carried her things into the house, then set up her laptop on the dining room table before going through her mail. A wedding invitation and two baby announcements. *Great.* It seemed all her friends back in New York were either getting married or having babies. At least being in Kansas gave her a good excuse to miss those celebrations that only served to remind her that she was alone.

She pushed the thought away and quickly got the coffee pot going, a dust rag flying, while Mozart provided background music for it all. The smell of fresh coffee wafted into the front parlor where Maddie was cleaning, and her spirits lifted. She put away the dust rag, filled a large mug, and set to work on her novel.

By the time the clock chimed eleven thirty, Maddie had nearly two thousand words to show for her diligence—along with a stiff spine. She stood to stretch. Her gaze traveled down the hallway to the ornate staircase that led to the upstairs guest rooms. She'd been dying to explore the rest of the house, but had been afraid to try the stairs on her sprained ankle. Gingerly she rotated her foot a few times and bent to rub it. The swelling was almost gone, the pain barely noticeable anymore. She'd dusted the entire first floor twice over the course of two weeks. Maybe it was time to see what kind of shape the second floor was in.

Thickly carpeted steps creaked under her weight, and she felt unaccountably guilty, as if she were snooping. But Mr. Tyler had said she was free to use any room in the house, so surely he wouldn't mind if she took a look around.

She was halfway up the stairs when the doorbell broke the silence and set Maddie's heart pounding. She crept back down the steps and peeked through the curtain at the windowed front door. Ginny Ross's Volkswagen sat in the driveway, and Ginny stood on the porch.

Maddie opened the door, feeling like a child caught snooping under the Christmas tree.

Ginny held out a white bag that bore the golden arches of McDonald's. "I hope you haven't had lunch yet. I brought cheeseburgers."

"Bless your heart! Let's go eat. I hadn't thought about it till now, but I'm starved, and all I brought was peanut butter."

"I can't stay too long. You have work to do, and I have a piano student coming early."

Maddie led the way to the dining room. She swept her books and papers to one side while Ginny opened the paper sack and took out two fat, wrapped burgers and a large order of fries. The savory scent filled Maddie's nostrils and made her stomach growl in protest. She went to the kitchen for paper napkins and glasses of ice water, gratefully tossing the dry sandwich from her lunch bag into the trash.

Maddie joined Ginny at the table, and the older woman bowed her head and blessed their food, ending with, "And please help Madeleine meet her deadline."

"Thank you, Ginny," Maddie said, deeply touched.

"So how *is* the book coming along?"

"Very well, I think. It's sometimes hard for me to tell. I get too close to my work to be objective. But I do know that if it weren't for this wonderful writing retreat you found for me, I'd still be limping along."

Ginny nodded. "Speaking of limping, your ankle seems to be better."

"Much better, thank you."

"And your sister's house? Are they making progress?"

"Slow, but sure," Maddie said over a mouthful of cheeseburger. She swallowed and wiped a spot of ketchup from the corner of her mouth. "To tell you the truth, Ginny, I'm almost dreading the day they finish."

"Why ever would you say that?"

"Because then I won't have an excuse to come to this lovely place anymore. There's just something. . .special about this house." She sobered. "But I know I'm imposing on Mr. Tyler. I don't want to overstay my welcome."

"Nonsense," Ginny said. "You're as welcome as you can be. Why just the other day Arthur was telling me how you've been doing the housekeeping. I think he's the one who's feeling guilty."

"It's nothing really. I just do a little dusting or sweeping each morning while I'm waiting for the coffee to brew."

"The way Arthur talks, it's a lot more than that. He wanted me to tell you that you are welcome to come for as many weeks as you need."

"Mr. Tyler sounds like the sweetest man. I wish I could meet him sometime. I'd like to thank him in person."

A strange twinkle came to Ginny's eyes. "Well, maybe we can arrange that one of these days."

Watching her neighbor, it struck Maddie that perhaps there was more than mere friendship between Ginny Ross and Arthur Tyler. How delightful to think of the lively Ginny having a romance. She'd never given the love lives of octogenarians much thought, but knowing Ginny the way she'd come to, suddenly she could picture it quite clearly. And if Ginny—at eighty-something—could find love again, maybe there was hope for Madeleine Houser somewhere down the road.

She banished the thought as quickly as it had come. Five years ago, after Rob Clevenger broke up with her, she'd decided once and for all that romance was much more trouble than it was worth.

Unfortunately Rob hadn't been the first to break her heart. It seemed marriage simply wasn't something God intended for her. She'd been blessed in many ways—with the warm relationship she had with her sister and her two nieces. With a successful career as a writer, and opportunities to travel all over the world. And now with Ginny's friendship. No, she should be satisfied and fulfilled with those things. Besides, she had Mom to take care of now. She didn't have time for romance.

"Don't you think so, Madeleine?" Ginny's voice interrupted her thoughts.

She had the decency to blush. "I'm sorry, Ginny. My mind drifted. What was that?"

Her neighbor leaned back and studied her for a moment. "I was just wondering if Arthur wouldn't be better off selling this house—the inn."

"I suppose it is an awful lot of work to keep the place up."

"Oh, it's not that. It's Annabeth. The memories must be thick here. They lived here their entire marriage, you know."

"No, I didn't know."

"Well, I, for one, think it's time he moved on. The man has a lot of good years left, and he's wasting them pining away for that woman. She was a dear woman—a dear friend––but she's gone, and he needs to accept it."

Maddie smiled to herself. She wondered if Ginny realized how transparent she was being.

After Ginny left, Maddie pondered the things the older woman had said, and an idea began to take root. Perhaps if Maddie met Arthur Tyler—got to know him a bit—she could spur things along between him and Ginny Ross. If Mr. Tyler was as obtuse in the ways of romance as the men she'd dated, he probably didn't have a clue Ginny had feelings for him. Hmm... Maybe there was the seed of a new novel in this. Her mind whirled with lovely possibilities that wove in and out of Anne Caraway's tale.

She scarcely looked up from her computer until the distant buzz of a lawnmower broke her concentration. She pushed back her chair and went to look out the parlor window. A husky, spike-haired teen in a baggy sweatshirt pushed a lawnmower back and forth across the front lawn. Maddie remembered Mr. Tyler mentioning in one of his notes that a high school student would be working in the yard on Fridays.

She went back to her keyboard and wrote steadily until the clock in the hallway chimed four. She packed up her things and wrote a little note to Mr. Tyler. She still wasn't quite comfortable calling the old gentleman Art, as he'd requested. She opted for *Arthur* instead.


*Dear Arthur,*
  *My thank-yous surely fall on deaf ears by now.*


Goodness, she hoped the man wasn't hard of hearing. She hadn't meant that literally. Ah, well, he was an English professor. Surely he could decipher her intent.

.  .  .

*But I simply cannot leave this wonderful house each day until I've properly thanked my unseen host.*

*Once again, I had a most productive day writing. Sometimes the peace and quiet here are so perfect I almost forget to take a break for lunch. Fortunately our dear, mutual friend remedied that today. Ginny Ross brought lunch out to the inn, and we had a wonderful visit. It made me realize I've been at my house so seldom over the past few days, I've missed the pleasure of having Ginny for a neighbor. I'm not sure I've ever met such a sweet, selfless woman— and so energetic! She runs circles around me.*

Maddie reread her words. She hoped her endorsement of Ginny wasn't too obvious. But then could one ever *be* too obvious with men? With a wry smile, she picked up the pen again.

*Ginny says you've given permission for me to come back next week. If you're certain that's not an imposition, I will happily take you up on the offer. The workers have made some progress on my house, but it's all going much slower than I imagined. At any rate, with the solitude I've found here at your inn, I'm finally beginning to believe I might make my deadline on this book after all. Thank you again, kind sir.*

*Have a nice weekend,*
*Madeleine Houser*

On the way home from the inn the following Monday, Maddie stopped by the post office to collect her mail. She'd had the mail from her New York apartment forwarded to Kansas, but it was slow in coming. Her mailbox had been depressingly empty recently. She bent and peered in the little windowed door. She had mail. She dug in her purse for the key. Her box yielded a bill from Mason Electric and a postcard saying she had mail too large for the box.

She took the card to the counter and handed it to the clerk. The man went back into the bowels of the building and returned a minute later with a manuscript-sized envelope sent with next-day postage. What was this? Surely Peggy hadn't finished proof-reading the last batch she'd sent already. She took the package out to the car and sliced it open with a nail file from her glove compartment.

Inside was the portion of her manuscript she'd sent to Peggy, ominously absent of red ink. A brief note lay on top under the wide rubber band that held the pages together:

*So sorry to return this, Madeleine, but I've taken a full-time job and will no longer be able to proofread for you. I tried to contact you before you mailed the manuscript, but I never got an answer at the number you gave me, and my e-mails aren't going through to you. I do hope this doesn't cause a problem.*

The implications of Peggy's note registered, and Maddie smacked the steering wheel with the flat of her hand. Electrical failures and water leaks and proofreaders quitting had conspired to keep her from turning this book in on time. She tossed the manuscript onto the pile of books and magazines in the passenger seat and put the key in the ignition. She really needed to go see her mother before she went home, but she wasn't sure she could handle one more depressing thing.

Tears came suddenly, and she wiped at them with the back of her hand. "Lord, I don't think I can take much more. Please just help me to get—"

A tapping sound on her car window broke through her prayer. She gave a little gasp, grabbed a tissue from the box on the floor, and dipped her head to dab discreetly at her cheeks before turning to roll down the window.

She didn't know the man bent beside her car, wearing an expression of deep concern. Wait. No, it was the handsome man who'd held the door for her at the post office last week.

"I'm sorry to bother you, but"––he gave an apologetic smile––"I couldn't help but notice you were upset. Is everything okay?"

Embarrassed as she was to have been caught crying, she was touched by the thoughtful gesture of this stranger—and a gorgeous stranger at that. Such intense blue eyes. He seemed familiar somehow. "I–I'm okay." She forced a smile. "I just got some bad news in the mail."

"Oh? I'm sorry. I hope it's nothing too serious. . . ."

"Oh no." She shook her head and affected a chuckle. "It's one of those things I'll probably laugh about in a few weeks, but right now it was just. . .too much. Thank you for asking, though. It was very thoughtful of you." She reached for the keys in the ignition, anxious to escape the man's sweet scrutiny.

He shrugged and ducked his head. "Sorry to have bothered you. I hope. . .I hope everything turns out okay."

"Don't worry. I'm sure it will."

He held up a hand in farewell and hurried across the street. In her rearview mirror, she watched him climb into an old Chevy pickup. She shook her head in wonder at the friendliness of these Midwesterners. No wonder Kate and Jed had loved raising their girls here in Clayburn.

Feeling oddly energized, Maddie drove to the nursing home and sat with her mother in the dining room while Mom picked at the bland food they served her. Her mother was quiet, but the vacant stare seemed less pronounced, and she even flashed Maddie a conspiratorial look of disgust when Mr. Bender slopped his coffee on the white linen tablecloth. Maddie headed for home feeling hopeful again.

When she unlocked the kitchen door and flipped on the light, she was delighted to see the cupboard doors back on their hinges and the floor cleaned off in preparation for laying the tile.

"Thank You, Lord." Maddie's whispered prayer echoed hollowly in the empty room.

As she walked through the house, she stopped in the living room in front of the old upright piano her nieces had practiced on. She leaned over the keyboard and played a tentative chord. The piano was sadly out of tune, but she scooted the bench out and sat down. Her rusty fingers explored the keys and soon found a simple melody she'd learned as a child. She hadn't brought her piano or any of her music with her from New York—not that she read music well anyway. She mostly played by ear. Now she plinked out the song, enjoying the mindless activity. The piano had always been good therapy for her.

Maddie played for half an hour, losing herself in the music. As her mind replayed the day, she smiled to herself, thinking of her neighbor's crush on Arthur Tyler, and scheming of ways to get Ginny Ross and the innkeeper together.

But the handsome face of the kind stranger at the post office kept intruding on her scheming.

Five

It was dark by the time Art finished his errands, and he stopped to grab a burger and fries to take home for supper. It'd been a long day--and it was only Monday. He'd been telling himself for a year now that he was going to retire from his teaching job. The commute was getting old, and with winter coming, it would be worse. But if he did retire, what on earth would he do with his time?

He could always start advertising the inn again and get it running back at full capacity. But since Annie's death, he hadn't had the heart for it. Still, it would beat driving an hour each way to work every day. He actually enjoyed the maintenance and odd jobs of keeping the inn up. He even rather liked cooking simple breakfasts for weekend guests. It was the little touches he'd never been good with. Those had been Annie's department--fresh flowers and scented candles, and clean linens on the beds in each room. That and cleaning the toilets and scrubbing the tubs. Those had been Annie's jobs too and she'd never once complained. He did those nasty jobs now, as best as he could, but he despised them.

Ms. Houser had inadvertently made it clear to him that he

had no clue what it took to keep up with the simple housekeeping of the place. What a difference it made simply to have the cobwebs swept away and the tabletops polished. If he had enough paying guests, he could hire someone to do those things.

The truth was, he could afford to hire someone now. Even after setting college funds aside for Annie's nieces, the inheritance she'd received when her parents died had made it possible for him to retire whenever he wanted.

But that was the trouble. He wasn't sure *what* he wanted.

Life had lost its sunshine, its certainty, when Annie left his world. It had been a long time since he'd felt passionate about anything. His friend Dave Sanders had suggested more than once that perhaps a change of place would provide the impetus he needed to jump-start his life. Maybe he did need to sell the inn and move away. But it was hard to imagine how leaving Clayburn —and his church, and the people he and Annie had come to love —could make his life more fulfilling.

He thought of Madeleine Houser. According to Ginny, the author had left her home in New York and moved to Kansas to be near her mother. If Art thought it would be difficult at his age, what must it be like for someone as. . .well as settled as Ms. Houser must have been in her life? Maybe he'd ask her about it. Their correspondence had deepened over the weeks she'd been coming to the inn to write, and the back-and-forth missives provided a bright spot in his otherwise mundane days.

Alex met him at the door, pawing at his legs, begging for a bit of hamburger. While Art and Alex shared supper, he tried to explain his dilemma in a note to the author.

*Dear Ms. Houser,*

*I have been contemplating something, and it struck me today that you might provide some insight on the topic.*

*Quite frankly, I have felt rather "stuck" since the death of my wife. Though I can hardly picture it, friends have suggested it might be wise to sell the inn and move away from Clayburn and all the memories it holds for me. Since you've just made the kind of move my friends are advising, I wonder how you feel about their suggestion. I don't want to burden you with the task of giving a floundering soul advice, but if you have any quick thoughts on the subject, I'd certainly be more than grateful for the input.*

*I trust the writing is still going well. Again, I deeply appreciate all the housekeeping you've done. The inn is wearing a much brighter face these days. And if there is anything I can do to make your stay here more comfortable or conducive to meeting your deadline, by all means, please let me know.*

*Happy writing,*
*Art*

He reread his note and had to smile at the formal tone he affected whenever he wrote to Madeleine Houser. Quite different from the terse, hip notes he scribbled on his students' essays. Perhaps it was only natural to pander to the sensibilities of one's audience, but reading this brief note reminded him of the long letters he'd written to Grandmother Tyler after he'd gone off to college.

He'd often asked his grandmother's advice—even, sometimes, when he'd already made up his mind about something. Like marrying Annie. It had been nice to have Grandmother confirm his decisions. On the rare occasion when Opal Tyler offered a dissenting opinion, Art had always given it careful consideration. His heart swelled at the memory.

He left the note lying on the table in the dining room where Ms. Houser would find it in the morning. It might be nice to meet Ginny's friend someday. Tell her how much Annie had enjoyed her books. Maybe he should read one of the woman's novels himself. According to Ginny, Madeleine Houser was quite well known in her genre.

There might even be a marketing angle to it--*Madeleine Houser wrote here.*--should he ever decide to advertise the inn again—provided, of course, Ms. Houser didn't mind him dropping her name in his brochures.

He doubted she would, though. Didn't most authors crave any publicity they could get?

Maddie read the note again, already composing a reply in her mind. She thought it rather odd that Mr. Tyler would ask advice of her, but she was glad for an opportunity to offer the inn's owner her opinion. Rubbing her chin thoughtfully, she picked up her pen.

*Dear Arthur,*

*First of all, if we're going to be on a first-name basis, it must be mutual. Please call me Madeleine.*

*I admit I feel a bit strange trying to offer you advice. Surely you are much wiser and more qualified than I to make such a decision. But I suppose I do have my own experience to share (and I'll try not to write a novel—ha!). Perhaps you'll find a nugget of help in hearing what I've gone through.*

*I was perfectly happy living in New York. But my sister's husband was transferred out of state, and my mother lives at the nursing home here in Clayburn. My sister convinced me that I could write anywhere. . .well, you know that story! At any rate, I made the move somewhat against my will and with an attitude that was less than Christian. For a while I let that attitude fester, and as you can imagine, things only got worse.*

*Once I finally started assuming God had a hand in this whole thing, I began to recognize many good things about the move. It caused me to step out of a box that had become a little too comfortable. Most of all, I'm happy to be near my mother during her final years. Even though Mom is in the latter stages of Alzheimer's and doesn't know me anymore, it's been a blessing to spend time with her. And then, of course, God put dear, dear Ginny in my life.*

*But enough about me. Since I don't know you or the reasons your friends are recommending this move, it's hard for me to give advice. I don't know where you stand in terms of faith, but I do know that Ginny has a deep respect for you, so perhaps you'll understand my perspective on this. I believe if you seek God about this matter, He will guide you to the right decision. It may not* seem *right at first. It may be difficult and lonely for a while, as my adjustment has been. But I have lived long enough to know that God can take a noxious weed patch and turn it into a sweet-smelling rose garden.*

Maddie started to sign off, tickled she'd found a way to campaign for Ginny again. But suddenly an idea came to her. She wondered why she hadn't thought of this before. She picked up the pen.

*Since you felt free enough to ask for my input, might I take the liberty of asking for yours? Last week I received the unfortunate news that I've lost my proofreader. I understand you teach English, and I wonder if you might know of someone among your associates who would be willing to do that sort of work for me. I have a wonderful editor at my publishing house, but what I need is someone to give my manuscript a once-over, checking for simple typographical and grammatical errors, inconsistencies in the story line. . .that sort of thing. It could even be a conscientious college student. If you know of someone who'd be willing to take on the task on rather short notice, I would be most appreciative. I have a January deadline that is beginning to terrify me! (Of course, I would expect to pay the going rate for the service.)*

*I'll be thinking of you as you mull over the decision facing you. And thank you in advance for any help you can provide regarding a proofreader.*

*Your friend,*
*Madeleine Houser*

Six

The following Monday Art locked the door to his office at the university and walked out to his parking space. His cell phone lay on the dusty seat of the truck, displaying a message notification. Dustin. He put the key in the ignition and listened to the voicemail.

Dustin Brevits, the high school kid who took care of the inn's lawn, was already overdue with the mowing. Now he'd gotten himself an after-school detention and was backing out on the responsibility again. Art punched the keypad and lobbed the phone onto the passenger seat. He had guests scheduled at the inn for Friday and Saturday nights. The recent rains and balmy weather had the grass growing as if it were summer again, and by the weekend it was going to look like a jungle.

He sighed. He'd just have to mow it himself. Not that he really minded the job, but it got dark so early these days he usually watched the sun set on the drive home. Maybe he could rearrange some office appointments and get home early enough on Friday afternoon to at least mow the main lawns. The flowers would have to go without a much-needed deadheading.

He could see why Ms. Houser had been so frustrated over her

lost proofreader. Nothing was more irritating than people who were not dependable. But––

Art slapped the ball of his hand to his forehead. He'd meant to post something on the job board in the English department about the proofreader job. Talk about unreliable!

But wait a minute. He'd been wanting to read one of Ms. Houser's novels anyway. Why didn't he offer to proofread it himself? Judging by her neatly penned notes, he doubted there would be much to mark on one of her manuscripts. Not to mention that he was beginning to feel rather guilty about the amount of housekeeping the woman was doing for him.

He'd walked through the house last night and rejoiced at how spotless it was. He wouldn't have to do a thing to the main floor before the guests arrived. He would, however, need to clean the third-floor guest room they'd reserved. Ms. Houser's cane undoubtedly had not allowed her to brave the steep stairway to the attic room.

With one hand on the steering wheel and one eye on the traffic, he rummaged in his briefcase for a notepad and pen, then jotted down some cryptic reminders to himself.

He pulled off of Hampton Road to the inn just as a beautiful Kansas sunset splashed across the western horizon. He parked the pickup, jumped out, and walked back to the mailbox, marveling at shades of pink and turquoise and tangerine he'd never seen any artist reproduce successfully. Walking back to the entrance to his basement apartment, the crunch of gravel beneath his feet echoed in the still fall air. How could he ever leave this place? Dave was crazy.

He threw his briefcase, jacket, and tweed cap on the cluttered table and went to check out the upstairs. Alex met him at the top of the steps with his comical half-purr, half-meow greeting. The dining-room table was empty. Hmmm. In the three-and-a-half weeks she'd been coming, Ms. Houser had failed to leave a note only one other time. Art checked the kitchen. She'd been here all right. The clean coffee carafe, a soup bowl, and a cup and saucer were neatly stacked in the dish drainer.

He was surprised at the wave of disappointment that swept over him at the absence of that note. Maybe Dave was right after all. Maybe he seriously needed to get a life.

Alex pattered after him as he climbed the carpeted stairs to the second floor and opened the door to the narrow stairwell that led to the attic suite the weekend guests had requested. This had been his and Annie's room before the inn had become so successful. Later, they'd decided to finish the basement apartment and open the suite to guests. Art let his hand rest on the brass doorknob for a moment, steeling himself. It was still difficult to enter this space that held so many sweet, intimate memories.

He flipped the light switch and climbed the steps. The air grew chill as he reached the top. He walked over to the antique dresser on the far wall. Fine dust coated the smooth oak surface, and the beveled mirror that hung over the dresser was dim with grime. He ducked under the low-hanging eaves and stepped into the modern bathroom adjoining the room. A bulb was out on the Hollywood strip lighting that surrounded the mirror. The window that looked out over milo fields to the north of the house was open an inch, and the sill was littered with dead flies. A tiny spider scurried down the drain of the large whirlpool tub. He made a mental note to bring up some cleaning supplies and bug spray after supper.

As he stepped back into the room and pulled the bathroom door shut behind him, his gaze fell on an oval frame, convex glass protecting the photograph inside. As much as he wanted to turn away, he was drawn to the picture like steel to a magnet.

The sepia-toned image looked as authentic as the antique frame—just as Annie had intended. But the stoic couple standing side-by-side in the photograph was Art and Annie Tyler, circa 2001. It had been taken on their Colorado honeymoon at one of those Old West novelty portrait places in Durango. Annie had picked out their costumes, including the handlebar mustache Art sported in the portrait.

Art ran his fingers over the glass, gently wiping the dust from the image. A lump came to his throat as he gazed through the glass into Annie's eyes. Though her expression was stern and posed—as the long exposure time of the old tintype cameras necessitated—Annie's eyes held a distinct twinkle.

He remembered the day as if it were yesterday. When he'd stepped from the dressing room wearing the Western duds and the dark mustache that matched his hair, Annie had dissolved in hysterical giggles. The photographer had a hard time capturing the serious pose Annie desired. But Annie had proudly framed the resulting print and penned the accompanying label, *Mr. and Mrs. Arthur Tyler,* in her flowing calligraphy.

Art shook his head to clear away the poignant memory. "Come on, Alex. We've got work to do."

Tail high, the cat followed him downstairs.

Maddie stared at the note, not quite sure how she should respond. Arthur Tyler had offered to proofread her manuscript. It would be wonderful to have an English professor read for her and especially helpful to get a male perspective on her story—even if that perspective did come from a generation or two before most of her readers were born. But how could she ask him for yet another favor? He'd already offered her so much. Still, she was desperate.

Before she could change her mind, she picked up her pen and accepted his offer as gracefully as she knew how.

*Dear Arthur,*

*I sincerely hope you aren't making your offer to proofread my manuscript out of some altruistic, chivalrous sense of duty. Though we've never met, I fear that is just the kind of thing you would do.*

*(Of course I use the word* fear *in a contrary sense. How I wish there were more men in my generation who possessed such a quality!)*

*I would love to take you up on your offer, under the following conditions:*

*1. You allow me to pay you a fair wage for your work.*

*2. You are brutally honest in your critique of my writing. (You would do me no favors by being kind!)*

*3. You feel free to drop the job at any time, for any reason, without explanation or guilt.*

*I will leave the first five chapters of my manuscript here, and if you are agreeable to these points, then have at it.*

*I know you must be weary of my gushing, but again, thank you so very much for all you've done to help me meet this deadline. You shall most definitely have a well-deserved mention in my acknowledgments page!*

*Have a lovely evening,*
*Madeleine Houser*

That task out of the way, she plugged her computer in and set to work. She finished chapter twenty-seven but found herself at a loss as to what should come next.

Standing to stretch her cramped muscles, she walked from room to room on the main floor, barely noticing the now-familiar and dear features of the house as she mulled over her story. No great insights came.

She had learned not to panic when this happened—though it was hard not to when she was so close to her deadline.

She paced the hallway that ran the length of the house, her sneakers making an annoying squeak with each step. As she came to the staircase in the foyer, she remembered that she'd never explored the second floor since the day Ginny had waylaid her with the enticement of cheeseburgers. Her novel temporarily forgotten, Maddie trotted up the stairs.

Three doors off the main hallway at the top of the landing stood open, and Maddie walked first into a sitting room, part of a suite decorated in a Victorian motif, ruffled and elegant with a wonderful old porcelain claw-foot tub in the bathroom.

The room adjacent to the suite was more austere, with its Art Deco oak furniture and wall coverings. She meandered slowly through each room and back again, lingering over the trinkets thoughtfully arranged atop the antique dressers and armoires. The rooms were much as she had imagined, fitting the style of the old Victorian home, yet with modern comforts seamlessly woven in. Obviously a great deal of loving care and no small measure of creative talent had gone into the decorating of these rooms.

Maddie actually grew excited, thinking of a whole new part of the house she could dust and polish. She would earn her keep yet.

As she went back into the hallway to go downstairs, another door—this one closed—caught her eye. She tried the painted brass knob and was surprised when it swung outward, revealing a narrow, carpeted stairway. Feeling like a trespasser, she climbed the steps, relieved to discover that the room at the top was another cozy guest suite. Stooping to peer out the dormered window at the head of the stairway, she gave a little gasp. The window overlooked a patchwork of Kansas fields, and a row of ancient cottonwood trees stood against a backdrop of sky the color of sapphires.

The majesty of New York City paled by comparison. Maddie knelt there for a long time, surprised again by how deeply this open sky and prairie landscape spoke to her spirit.

Finally she stood and explored the suite, delighted to find a low bookcase filled with her favorite authors. Her eyes widened as she spotted hardcover copies of her first four novels lined up on the bottom shelf. Ginny mentioned that Annabeth Tyler had been a fan. These must have been Mrs. Tyler's copies. The book jackets were in pristine condition, as though the books had never been read. But some people removed the jacket before they read a book.

She crossed the room and peeked into the large, modern bathroom, complete with whirlpool tub. Mr. Tyler must be expecting guests for the weekend, for the room sparkled. Every chrome fixture shone, and every wood surface glowed with a warm patina. The room still smelled of lemon oil and Pine-Sol. Maddie had begun to wonder if the inn ever had guests anymore, but here was her answer.

As she exited the bathroom, her gaze was drawn to an old portrait on the wall in front of her. A well-dressed young couple struck a staid pose, staring straight ahead. Maddie had seen similar photographs while researching her historical novels. It always fascinated her to see such ordinary, often oddly familiar faces staring back from the past, and this portrait was no exception. The convex glass encasing the photograph had the wavy quality typical of old glass, making it a bit difficult to see the portrait clearly. Still, the faces intrigued her—the glint of mischief so apparent in the woman's eyes. And the man reminded her of someone she knew. Or perhaps he was someone famous, someone she'd come across in her research once upon a time.

Her fascination grew when she read the label at the bottom of the frame: *Mr. and Mrs. Arthur Tyler*. Judging by their formal clothing, this might have been their wedding portrait. What a handsome young man Arthur Tyler had been. She could almost picture what he might look like now—the black curls and mustache grown white, the smooth planes of his face tanned like leather, crinkled with laugh lines. She could hardly wait to meet the man in person to see if her conjectures were accurate. If so, she could certainly understand Ginny's infatuation.

She cast about the room, hoping to discover a more recent portrait of the Tylers, but the only other frame in the suite held a faded, silvered mirror. Maddie studied her reflection for a moment, sweeping her hair up off her neck and twisting it into a wispy chignon like the one Annabeth Tyler wore in the portrait.

Glancing back at the portrait on the wall and the handsome figure the young Arthur Tyler cut, a strange ache of longing came over her.

All the heroes in her novels were men of centuries long past. Men of honor and integrity. Gentle men whose strength didn't depend on vulgarity and macho blustering. The only peers she'd met who had those qualities were spoken for. She let her hair fall limply to her shoulders and sighed.

But as she descended the stairs, an idea flickered. She'd been looking for a face for Jonathan Barlowe, the protagonist in her novel who would sweep her hapless heroine off her feet and into his heart. She had certainly found him. A smile pulled at the corners of her mouth. She wondered how Mr. Tyler would feel if she told him his portrait had provided a model for one of her characters. No. She didn't want to creep the man out. It must be her little secret for now. But she knew she would come up to this room each day to gaze into the eyes of her new hero before going back, inspired, to her computer. Ah, how she envied Anne Caraway.

rt thanked the postal clerk, slipped the new book of stamps into his shirt pocket, and started through the post-office door, stuffing his wallet into his back pocket as he walked. He glanced up in time to hold the door for an attractive young woman who was, like him, preoccupied, stuffing her gloves and keys into her purse. They almost collided, politely skirted around each other, then, in tandem, did a double take.

It was the woman from the white Mazda—the one he'd seen last week crying over some bad news the mail had brought.

Recognition sparked in her green eyes, and she flashed a little smile. "Oh, hi there." Her cheeks flushed a lovely shade of peach.

He didn't want to embarrass her, but took a risk, keeping his tone lighthearted. "You look considerably happier than the last time I saw you here."

The blush on her cheeks deepened. "Everything worked out fine." She looked up at him with a sheepish grin and started to say something, but stopped when Mabel Bachman, the elderly wife of Clayburn's mayor, shuffled toward them, weighed down with a bulky stack of packages.

Art hurried to hold the door open for the elderly woman.

Green Eyes gave a little wave and hurried on toward her car. By the time Art helped Mrs. Bachman with the door to the inner office, the Mazda was crawling down the street, headed north.

He felt strangely disappointed. He'd meant to introduce himself to the attractive stranger. Art didn't think she was married. No wedding ring. He'd noticed while she was stuffing her gloves into her bag. Somehow he couldn't picture a married woman driving that sporty Mazda—especially not with a passenger seat that looked like a filing cabinet and library rolled into one. Not that he planned to pursue this green-eyed beauty. She must be new to Clayburn. He'd never seen her before, and he knew just about everyone in town––by face, if not by name. He thought about asking around to see if any of his golf buddies knew who she was, but he could just hear the ribbing he'd get. As it was, his friends were constantly trying to set him up with some-body's cousin or stepsister or the former college roommate of a buddy's wife. No thank you. He did not want to go there.

Art drove home, fed Alex, and fixed a bologna sandwich, which he took upstairs to eat while he read Madeleine Houser's correspondence of the day. A sheaf of manuscript pages lay neatly on the dining-room table. Good. She must be agreeable to him proofreading her manuscript. He went into the kitchen for a drink, bending to peer out the kitchen windows as he ran fresh tap water over ice. Outside, the overgrown lawn rippled in the breeze. He made a mental note to remember to come home early enough on Friday to get it mowed before weekend guests arrived.

Back in the dining room, he read the note, smiling at the author's list of rules and her promise to list him in her acknowl-edgments for the book. He ran a hand through his hair. If the book turned out to be drivel, he might have to devise a graceful way to extricate himself from that dubious honor. He would never hear the end of it from his colleagues at the university if his name appeared on the acknowledgments page of a schmaltzy romance novel.

Brushing breadcrumbs from his hands, he pushed his sandwich plate away and drew the manuscript close. He pulled a pen from his shirt pocket. Alex jumped into his lap and turned a three-sixty to brush his tail across Art's nose before finally settling in.

"Hey, Buddy, what do you think? Am I going to like this lady's writing?" He stroked the cat's thick fur, and Alex revved his feline motor in response.

Running one hand absently down the length of the cat's back, Arthur Tyler began to read.

Friday morning, Maddie went out to the garage, loaded down with her computer bag and the reference books she would need. Her mind on a new scene for Anne Caraway's story, she turned her keys in the ignition. Nothing.

*Oh, great!* She tried again with the same results. Sighing, she got out of the car and went around to open the hood. She knew as much about car engines as she did about computers—zip. There didn't seem to be any smoke, nor were any liquids dripping or spewing, so she slammed the hood down and ran inside to call a mechanic.

An hour later, with her Mazda at Bud's Automotive and driving a monstrous old Buick compliments of Bud, Maddie headed west on Main.

She was already behind schedule, but she hadn't had the energy to see Mom the night before, so she stopped by the Clayburn Market and picked up a bouquet of rather sad-looking daisies and carnations and drove to the nursing home.

Mom was having another bad day, fidgeting and sputtering nonsensical syllables in a tired voice. She didn't seem to realize Maddie was there. Maddie stayed just long enough to transfer the flowers to an unbreakable vase and to visit briefly with the nurse.

She felt guilty about not spending more time with Mom, but what difference did it make when her mother didn't know her from the nurse's aide who came to deliver her breakfast tray?

She drove to the inn, feeling discouraged and depressed. But as soon as the old Victorian house came into sight, her spirits lifted. She tried not to think about how close the workmen were to finishing the remodeling on Jed and Kate's house. When the last tile was in place, she would have no excuse to come out here anymore.

Shaking off the thought, she let herself in, set up her computer, and immediately climbed the two flights of stairs to visit her new hero. The man behind the oval glass was as handsome as she remembered—as handsome as he'd been in her dreams.

Again, she was struck by how familiar he seemed. That often happened with her characters. She would have a vague picture of a character in mind, only to open up a catalog or magazine and see the perfect face staring back at her. She always clipped pictures of her characters for inspiration. But Anne Caraway's hero had been a long time making himself known. Maddie memorized the masculine contours of the young Arthur Tyler's face. The square jaw, the steel gaze of his pale eyes. Though she couldn't tell from the sepia-toned photograph, she imagined his eyes to be a mesmerizing shade of blue-gray. Oh, to have been born a few decades earlier!

She studied Annabeth Tyler's image—the playful glimmer in her eyes, the love on her face so tangible and compelling. Inspired, Maddie hurried downstairs to capture that passion on the computer screen.

She typed steadily, breaking for a quick cup of coffee and a bagel she'd bought that morning at Clayburn's newly opened Main Street Deli. The story flowed, and finally Maddie could visualize the perfect ending. She made her fingers fly across the keyboard, eager to finish her tale so she could reread it and add in the subtle nuances of detail and characterization that imbued her stories with her own unique style.

Shortly after three o'clock, the sound of a motor revving outside startled her. Oh, that's right… This was the day that high school kid mowed the lawn. Her concentration broken, she pushed back her chair and stood to stretch and knead the kinks from her spine.

She walked through the hallway into the front parlor and pushed the heavy curtains aside. Though he had his back to her, Maddie could see that the person pushing the mower wasn't the spike-haired teen who usually came. This guy had shiny black hair that curled slightly at the nape of his tanned neck. And he was older—late thirties, Maddie guessed. Tall and slender, but even beneath the long-sleeved T-shirt he wore, she could see taut muscles flex as he maneuvered the push mower across autumn-brittle grass.

As the man reached the edge of the driveway and turned the mower toward the house, she took in a sharp breath and let the curtain fall back over the window. She knew that man. It was the guy from the post office. The one who'd caught her crying over Peggy's returned manuscript.

Cautiously, she pulled the curtain aside and peered out again. She watched him for a while. But when she went back to the dining room and sat down at her computer, she'd lost her focus. She kept thinking about the handsome man from the post office. The same man mowing the lawn. She tried not to acknowledge the disappointment she felt at discovering he apparently was employed doing odd jobs. Not only was it small-minded and judgmental of her, but she was jumping to conclusions.

"Besides," she said under her breath, "you're not in the market for a man, Houser. Remember?" An odd nagging nudged the back of her mind—something she couldn't quite put her finger on.

Finally she heard the lawn mower's engine cut off and a few

minutes later the sound of tires crunching on the gravel drive. She looked at the clock over the stairwell. It was time to leave anyway.

She'd toyed with the idea of staying until Mr. Tyler came home some night. She could finally meet the man and perhaps put in a good word for Ginny. But tonight wasn't the time for that. Seeing the stranger from the post office here at the inn had left her feeling oddly disconcerted. She just wanted to go home and hibernate.

Art delivered the lawn mower to Mike and Milt's Sharpening Service and drove back to the inn. When he pulled into the drive, he saw that Madeleine Houser's old Buick was gone. The inn looked neat and tidy, sitting on the freshly cut lawn, and Art admired his handiwork with satisfaction. If the weather cooperated, he could pick up the mower next week and park it in the garage, sharpened and ready to go for a new season. But if this Indian summer persisted, he'd probably have to cut the grass at least once more before it went dormant.

He'd rather enjoyed the task of mowing. The physical exertion, the sun on his face, and an October breeze cooling his skin gave him a feeling of gratification and. . .was it hope?

The verse from Genesis 8 that Pastor Rennick had read last Sunday floated through his mind: "While the earth remains, seedtime and harvest, and cold and heat, and summer and winter, and day and night shall not cease." Of course, the verse referred to God's promise to Noah that He would never again destroy the earth by a great flood.

Still, as Art looked north across the highway to the ripening milo fields and the trees in their autumn glory, he felt the hope of God's promise bloom in his heart. Tragic things happened. Yet in the midst of them, if one were watchful, he could see God's beauty manifested just as it was in the gold and russet of the dying leaves. Life went on, and God had given him strength and courage to keep living. The assurance of tomorrow, of a new harvest in the field, of springtime after a long winter.

Even after Annie.

Art got his weekend guests checked in and settled in their rooms, and after dinner, with Alex comfortably ensconced in his lap, Art settled into his recliner with Madeleine Houser's manuscript on his knee, a red pen at the ready. The pen mostly remained capped, however, for Art was captivated by the story. He had read two chapters the afternoon before and was immediately impressed—and sheepishly contrite over his premature judgment of Ms. Houser's writing. Now well into the third chapter, he was amazed at the way the author made him believe the book had actually been written in 1871. And yet she'd found the balance of speaking to the sensibilities of the contemporary reader as well. It was a rare thing.

The woman had obviously done her research. The historical details were sharply accurate. Her portrayal of the Chicago fire was chilling. He could almost hear the flames from the great conflagration crackling and snapping around him. And her characterizations were multilayered, with intricately woven relationships that kept him turning pages. He especially liked the hero. Not usually one for love stories, he found himself intrigued by Jonathan Barlowe and could easily identify with this flawed man.

He stopped reading only long enough to scribble a note to Madeleine Houser.

*I am enthralled by your story, Ms. Houser. I had no idea what I've been missing all these years. I will finish these five meager chapters you've left me long before bedtime, and then I face the prospect of an entire weekend not knowing the fate of Anne Caraway, precocious little Charlie, and, of course, the quintessential hero, Jonathan*

*Barlowe. (Please do not tell me you are one of those cruel writers who kill off beloved characters for no good reason.)*

Art drew a happy face beside that last sentence, lest she take offense—or lest she *was* one of those cruel writers. He signed his brief note, picked up the manuscript, and was soon transported again to Chicago, 1871.

*Eight*

By the following Monday morning, Maddie had her Mazda back—complete with a new battery and spark plugs, plus a bill for nearly two hundred dollars. But the car ran like a top. She packed up her computer and books along with a couple of granola bars to take to her mother before going out to the inn. The tile crew had finally arrived, and she had to skirt around the beefy father-son team and their assorted toolboxes to reach the back door. She'd almost made her escape when the telephone rang.

"Could I speak to Madeleine Houser, please?"

"Yes, this is Madeleine."

"Arthur Tyler. . .from Annabeth's Inn? Is this Madeleine *Houser,* the author?" The low, gravelly voice was just as Maddie had imagined Arthur Tyler would sound.

"Oh, yes, Mr. Tyler. Hello! So nice to talk to you."

The muffled sound of hoarse coughing, then, "I apologize. I seem to be coming down with something. I was wondering. . .were you planning on working at the inn today?"

"Well, yes... I was. But I certainly wouldn't have to. I could make other plans..." She tried to sound cheery despite her chagrin at the prospect.

"No. No. Please come ahead. I just wanted to let you know that I'm staying home in bed. Didn't want you to be alarmed if you heard noises coming from the apartment below. I—"

"Oh, I don't want to disturb you. Maybe it would be best if––"

"No. Please. I'm not trying to discourage you from coming at all. Judging by the way I feel right now, I'll probably sleep all day. I'll have no reason to leave my apartment, and it won't bother me one bit to have someone there. I'm used to having guests overhead. I just wanted to warn you that someone would be downstairs, that's all... in case you hear me rattling around down there."

The younger half of the tile-laying crew pounded a rubber mallet on the floorboards and sang off-key with his iPod. Maddie held her breath. She would get exactly nothing written if she stayed home and tried to work in this zoo. "If you're sure?" she said into the phone.

"Quite sure. Please, make yourself at home." Mr. Tyler cleared his throat again and gave a gruff chuckle. "I might warn you, though, I'm calling dibs on the famous foot-warming cat today."

Maddie laughed into the receiver. "I understand completely. It sounds like you need Alex's services worse than I do."

She put the phone back in its cradle and stared at it, unseeing. Because of the photograph in the attic bedroom, Maddie had a distinct image of Arthur Tyler—even if it was a half century old. She felt she knew him through the delightful notes he left for her, but it was strange to now have a voice to put to those notes. He had almost become like one of her characters—an intangible, yet beloved presence in her life. But hearing his throaty voice had made him seem all too real, and suddenly she felt very odd about going out to the inn, knowing he would be downstairs in his apartment.

The clatter of a slamming toolbox lid brought her to her senses. Mr. Tyler was expecting her, and she didn't want to call him back and risk disturbing him. Climbing over the flooring materials that littered the kitchen, she grabbed her things and made her escape.

On a whim, she stopped by the Main Street Deli and picked up two take-out tubs of chicken noodle soup. She'd heat up one for lunch and leave the other in the refrigerator for Mr. Tyler. That ought to be good for what ailed him, and it was another small way she could show her appreciation.

Arthur Tyler set his cell phone carefully on his bedside table, flipped off the lamp, and sat in bed, staring at the opposite wall. *Odd.* If he didn't know better, he'd have thought the woman he'd just spoken to was someone younger. Much younger.

But with his sinuses so clogged, his hearing was probably distorted. He shook his head and reached for a tissue, then blew his nose so loudly that Alex leapt from his nest at the foot of the bed and hissed.

"It's okay, Buddy. Go back to sleep." Art stroked the gray-and-white fur that now stood comically on end.

The cat turned two full circles, plopped back on the bed, and resumed purring. Art tucked his feet into the warm spot the cat provided, slid beneath the fluffy down comforter, and drifted into a Nyquil-induced haze.

He awakened some time later to the sound of footsteps--decidedly feminine ones--overhead. Alex jumped off the bed and trotted down the hallway to investigate. Art glanced at the clock on the bedside table. 8:45. That would be Madeleine Houser. His head throbbed. Stifling a cough, he shrank under the covers.

He heard Alex pad softly up the stairs, then the youthful voice from the telephone cooing and clucking at Alex. There went his foot warmer. *Traitor.*

Curious, he crept out of bed and went to the foot of the stairs. He heard the refrigerator open and close, then the sound of water running and the coffeemaker beginning its cycle. With his stuffy nose he couldn't smell the brew, but he sure wouldn't have minded a cup. It would feel great on his scratchy throat.

He was tempted to throw a sweatshirt over his T-shirt and sweatpants and go up to introduce himself. But he dare not expose her to this nasty bug. At her age, a virus like this could easily turn into pneumonia.

Instead, he went to his kitchenette and boiled a mug of water in the microwave. He scooped in two spoonfuls of stale instant coffee and stirred. Wholly unsatisfying, but it would have to do. Someday he'd break down and buy a coffeemaker for the apartment.

He heard Ms. Houser talking upstairs again, presumably to his faithless feline. Carrying the steaming mug, he walked over to the partition between the stairway and his living area, careful to stay out of sight in case the woman should be at the top of the stairs. He didn't want to give her a heart attack.

"Come on, kitty," he heard her say. "Go on. Get back down there. You need to stay with your master today. Go on, Alex. I don't have anything for you."

How sweet. She was trying to coax Alex back downstairs. He liked this lady. And her voice—something about it struck a chord with him. It had a musical quality with the faintest hint of the East Coast in her accent. He was having trouble making that voice match the picture of the author he'd formed in his mind.

Feeling light-headed and groggy, Art went to his room and crawled back under the covers. He drifted off to sleep, thinking how nice it was to have someone upstairs puttering around in the kitchen and making use of his poor, neglected home.

Maddie had a hard time concentrating, knowing Arthur Tyler was practically right beneath her. Several times she heard his deep, wracking cough and was tempted to heat up the chicken soup she'd brought and take it down to him. But she didn't want to embarrass the man by catching him in his bathrobe—or worse.

She ignored Alex and focused on editing the chapter she'd written the day before. Finally the cat sauntered back downstairs.

At noon, she heated up a container of the soup. Careful as she was to tread lightly, the floors in the old house creaked with every step. It was a wonder Mr. Tyler didn't storm up the stairs and ask her to leave.

At two o'clock, having accomplished painfully little, she packed up her laptop and books. Before leaving, she composed a brief note.

*Dear Mr. Tyler,*

*I'm so sorry you're ill. I hope I didn't disturb you too much today. It was probably a bad idea for me to come here with you home sick. I'm afraid every creak and squeak in the house must have sounded like a herd of camels to you. I do apologize and hope you're feeling better by the time you read this. I've left you some of the new deli's wonderful chicken noodle soup. As you may know, studies show that chicken soup actually has medicinal value for cold sufferers. I hope you enjoy it. Even if it doesn't cure what ails you, it is delicious.*

*Perhaps it would be best if I don't come back to the inn until you let me know you are well and able to return to work.*

*Praying for your speedy recovery,*
*Madeleine Houser*

*P.S. I apologize for "stealing" Alex away from you for a while this morning. I hope you don't think I enticed him with kitty treats or anything. I promise you, he came of his own accord.*

·   ·   ·

She drew a smiley face after her postscript and signed the note.

Driving home, she fought discouragement at losing a whole day of writing. She simply must learn to discipline herself to work under adverse conditions.

When she pulled into her drive a few minutes later, Ginny Ross was next door sweeping the first of autumn's offerings off her front porch. Maddie parked in the garage and went around to the front of the house to talk with her neighbor.

"Well, hello there, Miss Madeleine." Ginny wielded her broom to scoot a giant red maple leaf onto the grass.

Maddie eyed the broom, then looked up into the branches of oaks and maples that had yet to shed their autumn coats. "That's kind of a losing battle, don't you think?"

"Oh, I know it is, but it's good exercise. Besides, I enjoy being out of doors on a day like this."

"Glorious weather," Maddie agreed.

Ginny leaned the broom against the porch railing. "So, how many words did you write today?"

Maddie sighed. "Not very many, I'm afraid. Mr. Tyler was home sick and I couldn't concentrate."

"Arthur was at home?" A strange expression crossed Ginny's face. "Did you meet him?"

"No. He was in bed sick. The poor man has a terrible cough."

Ginny clicked her tongue. "Oh my. I don't suppose that was very conducive to a quiet day of writing."

"It's not that so much... It just felt strange to be in his house with him right downstairs."

Ginny didn't respond but picked up the broom and started sweeping again.

"Have you made plans for dinner yet, Ginny? Let me take you out to eat at the new deli."

"Oh, you don't need to do that, honey."

"I know I don't need to, but I'd like to."

"Well, I have been wanting to try out the deli..."

"It's settled then. Six o'clock?"

"Sounds great. Just toot your horn when you're ready. I'll meet you in the driveway." Ginny resumed sweeping, and Maddie imagined there was a livelier lilt to her friend's step.

"Well, I hate to admit it, but this chicken noodle soup is almost as good as mine." Ginny dipped into her bowl for another spoonful of the rich broth. She sat across from Maddie in a cozy booth at the Main Street Deli.

Maddie smiled and buttered a slice of wheat toast. "Well, yours must be wonderful then." An idea leapt into her brain, and she gave it voice, trying to sound matter-of-fact. "Ginny, you should make some of your homemade soup for Mr. Tyler. That ought to cure what ails him." It was the perfect opening Maddie had been seeking to get the two together. Ginny didn't need to know that she'd already taken Art some of the deli's soup.

Ginny nodded, eyes glistening. "Maybe I'll just do that. You could take it to him when you go tomorrow."

Maddie's head came up and she scrambled for a way to get her plan back on track. "Well...actually, as long as he's not feeling well, I'll probably work from home. I don't want to disturb him. But *you* could go and—"

"Nonsense!" Ginny said. "If you come bearing food, he certainly can't complain. Besides, I'd say it's high time you two met."

Feeling caught in a trap she'd set herself, Maddie didn't argue.

Ginny phoned early Tuesday morning to say she'd been asked to help with a funeral dinner at church, and that Arthur Tyler's chicken soup would have to wait a day. Grateful for the reprieve,

Maddie spent the morning at home doing laundry and tidying up the house as best she could with the flooring guys in the kitchen.

The housework done, she called her editor in New York to discuss some questions that had come up as she wrote. Janice was talkative and enthusiastic, and Maddie hung up feeling encouraged. It *was* rather nice to take a day off from writing. Her story still perked quietly in the background, and she had a feeling that when she got back to her computer the words would flow.

She spent the afternoon sitting with her mother in the nursing home's large sunroom. Maddie had brought her mother's Bible and read quietly to her from the worn volume. She didn't know if Mom understood or even heard the words anymore, but Maddie had discovered the Scriptures often seemed to calm her mother's restlessness. And her own, as well.

She read aloud from 1 Corinthians 13. " 'But when the perfect comes, the partial will be done away. When I was a child, I used to speak as a child, think as a child, reason as a child; when I became a man, I did away with childish things. For now we see in a mirror dimly, but then face to face; now I know in part, but then I shall know fully, just as I also have been fully known.' "

Was this how it was for Mom? Seeing the world as if through a dim mirror? Yet the passage wasn't written only for people with dementia. Maddie's own vision was dark compared to what it would be when she saw Jesus face to face. Mom's mind had been ravaged by a horrible disease, yet her spirit waited for release, waited to soar to her Savior. It was an amazing thought.

She closed the Bible and patted her mother's cold hand. "I love you, Mom."

They sat together in silence for a long while, and Maddie tried to enjoy simply being in her mother's presence.

Shortly before five, a white-uniformed nurse's aide appeared in the wide doorway. "Mrs. Houser? Are you ready to go to the dining room?"

Mom fingered the crocheted hem of her sweater, not looking up. Maddie put a hand gently on her arm. "Mom, it's time for dinner. Shall we go to the dining room?" Her mother looked into her eyes but no recognition lit her gaze. Maddie dismissed the nurse's aide with a little wave. "I'll walk down with her."

Taking the frail hands in hers, she stood and gently pulled her mother up beside her. Maddie attempted to match the shuffling gait Alzheimer's had bestowed, and together they started down the long corridor.

Nine

Before the workmen arrived the next morning, Maddie heard Ginny's cheery greeting sail through the back door. The savory aroma of chicken broth wafted through the house, and Maddie followed the scent into the kitchen.

"Well, good morning." Ginny set the pot of soup on a dish towel on the kitchen table and looked around the room, taking in the newly laid tile and the granite countertops. "This is coming along nicely."

"I'm beginning to believe there might be light at the end of the tunnel." Maddie ran her hand over the smooth surface of the counter. "The guy who's doing the counters can't finish up until next week, but he thought he'd be done in a couple of days. The only thing left then is some touch-up paint."

"And then you won't need to go to the inn anymore," Ginny said. "I suppose it'll be a relief not to have to lug your things back and forth every day."

"Yes, I suppose it will." She was surprised at how gloomy the thought made her feel. Maybe after she got the new kitchen cleaned up and all her dishes put away, she'd feel differently. But when would she ever find the time?

"I'd better let you get going." Ginny gave the soup pot a proprietary pat. "Tell Arthur all he needs to do is put this on the stove until it's warm. I don't want him boiling all the flavor away. Or maybe you could heat it up for him, Maddie? Help yourself to a bowl."

Ginny turned when she got to the back door, a wily glint in her eyes. "There's plenty there for both of you. You could have lunch together."

"Oh, well...thank you. I'm sure Mr. Tyler will appreciate it." She tried to hide her dismay. If Ginny kept this up, Maddie would soon be spoon-feeding the old gentleman.

Her neighbor flapped her hands like a mother hen directing chicks. "Go on now. Don't let me keep you."

When Maddie turned onto Hampton Road a few minutes later, soup in tow, she wondered what in the world she'd gotten herself into.

Art heard a car on the driveway and sat up in bed, disoriented. He'd tossed and turned all night long—burning up one minute and shivering the next. He reached for a tissue on the nightstand and blew his nose. This bug had laid him low, but it seemed his fever had finally broken.

The gravel crunched, and the car came to a stop. Madeleine Houser must have decided to come after all. He swung his legs over the side of the bed and went to the kitchenette to heat some water for coffee. He wished he'd gotten up in time to brew a pot of real coffee upstairs before she arrived.

He went to the view-out window overlooking the drive. Expecting to see Ms. Houser's old Buick in the drive, he was surprised to see a white Mazda.

His heart lurched. Had he scheduled guests for today and forgotten about it? He tried to think where he'd seen that car before. Someone was moving around inside the vehicle, but he couldn't tell who or how many.

Pulling on a pair of blue jeans, he flew up the stairs to the main floor, and went to the desk in the parlor where he kept the appointment calendar. His head pounded as he flipped through the bookings, trying to remember what day it was. Wednesday. But no guests scheduled until the weekend.

The sound of a key turning in the front door mere feet from where he stood shot adrenaline through his veins. That would be Madeleine Houser. Strange, he hadn't heard *her* car drive in.

Glancing up at the antique mirror over the parlor desk, he caught sight of his reflection. *Good grief.* Two days' worth of black stubble sprouted from his jawline, his hair spiked out in forty different directions, and his nose would give Rudolph a run for his money. He'd frighten the poor woman to death!

He clapped the appointment book shut and raced back through the house, practically diving down the stairs to his apartment. Out of breath with his heart thumping in his ears, Art draped himself over a bar stool in the kitchenette. Above him, the front door closed, and quiet footsteps echoed from the entry.

A repeat of Monday morning's litany of sounds began—a computer being turned on, water running into a carafe. What on earth...? Had she sent the visitor in the Mazda away?

Soon the coffeemaker was chugging and hissing. His sinuses were considerably less stuffy today, and the delicious aroma tickled his nose.

The footsteps retreated through the house and back out the front door. Maybe she was going to talk to the driver of the Mazda. Curious, Art returned to the window and watched. No sign of Ms. Houser's Buick--or Ms. Houser--but the white Mazda was still parked in the driveway. The driver—a woman— had gotten out and was bent over, taking something from the backseat.

A brisk breeze kicked up, and she struggled to hold the car door open with one knee while she tugged on something in the car. Finally she stood and turned to face the house, cradling a large cooking dish of some sort. The wind whipped her hair in her face, and she flipped her head back, trying unsuccessfully to shake the thick mane out of her eyes. She turned slightly and gave the car door a shove with one hip—one very shapely hip, he couldn't help but notice.

Where had Ms. Houser disappeared to? The woman turned and started up the front walk. In that instant, something clicked in his brain. The white Mazda. Of course! It was the woman from the post office—the lovely Miss Green Eyes.

Coming up his walk.

His next breath came in a tight wheeze. What in the world was she doing here? And why was she bringing food?

He wasn't about to answer the door. Not in his condition.

But where *was* Madeleine Houser? He was sure he'd heard her go out just moments ago. Maybe she would tell Green Eyes he was indisposed.

He looked out on the drive again. The Buick was nowhere to be seen. But why would Ms. Houser set up her computer, make coffee, and then leave? It made no sense. Unless she'd forgotten something and run home for it. That must be it.

Art listened for the doorbell. Instead, he heard the front door open and the floorboards above him creak. He leaned against the wall that concealed the stairway. He heard the refrigerator open and close, the sound of coffee being poured, and soon the steady click of a computer keyboard. What was going on?

Alex slipped past him and scurried up the steps.

"Well, hello there, Alex," a familiar voice cooed. "Are you being a bad boy again? You're going to get me in trouble, you know. Now you go on. Get back down there and keep Mr. Tyler's feet warm."

Art closed his eyes and lifted his chin toward the ceiling. *Tyler, you idiot! How could you be so dumb?*

On impulse, he hurried to the bedroom and threw open Annie's side of the closet. Annabeth's sister and nieces had helped him pack up Annie's clothes and shoes more than a year ago, but two shelves in the back of the closet still held part of her beloved collection of books. Art knelt in front of the shelves and ran his fingers along the titles, looking frantically for one particular volume.

There it was. *Hope's Song*, by Madeleine Houser.

Art slipped the book from the shelf, knowing what he would find even before he opened the cover. He turned the book over, opened to the back flap of the dust jacket, and stared at the photograph.

A familiar pair of mesmerizing green eyes stared back at him.

The beautiful young woman at the post office—the one who'd made his heart beat a little faster—was Madeleine Houser. Green Eyes was the author of the compelling novel in which he'd immersed himself for the past few nights. This lovely creature--the one who'd penned the delightful notes Art had so looked forward to each evening--was Ginny's friend. Ginny's *young* friend. And she'd spent nearly every day of the past month in this very house—*his* house!

How could his perceptions have been so ridiculously off-base? What happened to the gray-haired old lady? The one who walked with a cane and drove an old monster of a Buick?

Why hadn't Ginny *told* him? Yet...what had there been to tell? Ginny couldn't know he was infatuated with the lovely stranger at the post office. He looked at Madeleine Houser's publicity photo on the book jacket again. If he had only taken Ginny's advice, he would have read one of Ms. Houser's books and put two and two together long ago.

Art fell back against the bed and sat with his head in his hands, laughing softly to himself as each intricate facet of this great deception—one he'd apparently manufactured in his own mind—came to light.

Twenty minutes later, he felt a brush of soft fur against his bare arm. "Alex, you rascal. You knew all along, didn't you?" He chuckled and scratched the cat under the chin, then hauled himself off the floor and went down the hall to the bathroom.

It was time to shower and shave and properly introduce himself to the lovely, talented—and ever so young—Madeleine Houser.

Maddie heard the sound of running water downstairs. Mr. Tyler must be up and around. Maybe he would come upstairs and she could offer to warm some of Ginny's soup for him. That ought to make her neighbor happy.

She felt rather excited and just a bit nervous at the prospect of finally meeting her mysterious host—and the hero of her novel. But of course she wouldn't mention that. A flush of heat crept up her neck at the thought.

She skimmed through her latest chapter for typos, then went into the kitchen to put Ginny's soup on to heat. If Mr. Tyler didn't come up, maybe she'd get up the courage to take a bowl down to him. Compliments of Ginny, of course.

She found a package of soup crackers in a basket on top of the refrigerator and fixed a tray with a cloth napkin and a glass of ice water. On a whim, she went out to the front porch, and plucked one of the faded roses from the bush near the railing. She placed it in a tiny bud vase she found in a cupboard. Surveying her handiwork with satisfaction, she stirred the soup once more and listened for sounds of life downstairs.

The water had stopped running, but all was quiet below. Maybe he'd gone back to bed. She certainly didn't want to wake him. Not sure what to do, she turned the heat down under the soup and went back to try to write another scene in her novel.

A few unproductive minutes later, Alex's meow caused her to look up from her computer. Footsteps sounded on the stairway not ten feet from where she sat. Ah, he *was* awake. She was finally going to meet the elusive Arthur Tyler. Sitting straighter in her chair, she slipped off her glasses, moistened her lips, and tucked her hair behind her ears.

But the head that appeared over the railing did not belong to Arthur Tyler. It was. . .the lawn guy. The man from the post office. Maddie took in a sharp breath, mildly alarmed that he had just walked into the house without knocking.

"Oh! Hello," she said, trying to appear calm. She pushed back her chair and stood, glad for the massive oak table between them. "Are you here to mow the lawn?" She motioned toward the front of the house.

"The lawn?" The man stared at her as though she were speaking Swahili.

"Um. . .Mr. Tyler is home sick today," she explained. "He's downstairs. I–I can get him if you like."

The man's bemused gaze made her extremely uncomfortable. "Madeleine?"

Maddie gulped. *How did he know her name?* And today wasn't the day the lawn guy usually came. Her heart beat erratically and she struggled for a breath.

The man came up the last two stairs to the landing, and Maddie took a step back, bumping into the chair behind her.

He put a hand to his chest. "Ms. Houser, *I'm* Arthur Tyler."

"Wh–what?" What kind of nut case *was* this guy?

"I'm sorry if I frightened you." He shook his head. "And I am home sick today. I–I don't think I'm contagious anymore. I just thought it was time I introduced myself." He waited, looking at her with something like amusement in his eyes.

"You're Arthur Tyler? But I thought. . ."

"Yes, I'm Art Tyler. You thought I was someone else?"

Maddie reached behind her, felt for the brocade seat of the straight-back chair, and crumpled onto it. "I'm sorry. I'm. . .a little confused right now. I thought. . ." The truth began to unfold in her mind, and she giggled. "Well, I thought you were. . ."

He waited, dark brows knit together.

She started again. "For some reason, I assumed you were

Ginny's friend. Well, I know you *are* her friend, but I thought you were Ginny's age. I thought you were *old.*" She knew she was rambling, but her brain was having trouble wrapping itself around the now obvious truth.

Arthur Tyler threw back his head and laughed. "You thought *I* was old?" he said, when he finally caught a breath. "I thought the same thing!"

"You thought you were old?" Maybe he *was* a nut case after all.

He laughed again. "No, no. I thought *you* were old. Ginny said she had this writer friend and I just jumped to conclu—"

"Apparently we both jumped to some conclusions." Her mind whirled, trying desperately to sort out this whole outrageous scenario.

"Yes," Arthur said, a hint of suspicion creeping into his voice, "and I don't recall our friend Ginny doing anything to correct those misperceptions."

Maddie thought for a minute, remembering the mischievous gleam in Ginny's eye earlier that morning. "You're right. I'm sure I said something that would have let her know I thought—wait a minute! And to think I was trying to—" She stopped, feeling herself blush.

"What?"

Maddie giggled again. "I was trying to set you and Ginny up. I thought she had a crush on you. But all this time—"

Arthur Tyler took a step toward her and a light of recognition came to his eyes—eyes that, up close, were exactly the shade of blue-gray Maddie had imagined.

"Ginny Ross was trying to set *us* up? Is that it?"

Maddie smiled and nodded slowly, remembering her neighbor's insistence that Maddie deliver the chicken soup in person. "I have a feeling that's exactly what she was up to."

Arthur pulled a chair out from the dining-room table, turned it around, and straddled it, resting his arms on the high back.

"Well, isn't this one for the books? No pun intended." He grinned, looking for all the world like Jonathan Barlowe.

They sat looking at one another, shaking their heads. Finally Arthur unfolded his lean body from the chair, rose, and stretched out a hand. "Madeleine Houser, I'm Arthur Tyler. I'm very pleased to finally meet you. The *real* you."

Maddie took his hand, smiling broadly. "And I'm pleased to meet you, too, kind sir. After all our correspondence, I–I wish I could say, 'I feel like I know you,' but I'm so confused right now, I'm afraid that wouldn't be altogether true."

"No," he laughed. "Not for me, either." He dipped his head. "But I'd certainly like to remedy that."

*Ten*

The kitchen smelled of chicken broth and coffee and the slightest hint of some delicate, feminine cologne. After being without his olfactory senses for several days, Art inhaled each scent with fresh appreciation.

He smiled at the woman sitting across from him and spooned another bite of the fragrant soup into his mouth. "Mmm. . .this is wonderful," he said over a mouthful of noodles. "I think I feel better already. I can see why they say this stuff has medicinal value," he added with a wink.

"Well, I'd say this goes down a bit easier than any medicine." Madeleine Houser dabbed at the corner of her mouth with a paper napkin.

For a few minutes the two ate together in silence—a remarkably comfortable silence, given the fact they'd met only twenty minutes ago.

Yet watching her, Art felt he knew the soul of the beautiful woman sitting at his table. His heart swelled at the amazing discoveries they'd made. To think they'd each had such skewed perceptions of the other. Every time he thought of the comedy of errors that had brought them to this moment, he wanted to laugh out loud.

Madeleine looked up and caught him watching her, but the quirk of her shapely lips told him she was having similar thoughts.

"So all this time you've imagined me as a doddering old man?"

"Not exactly doddering." She tilted her head. "I was thinking more along the lines of distinguished and. . .dapper."

Art was charmed by the blush of crimson that climbed her throat.

"I wish I could give parallel adjectives for the picture I had of Ms. Madeleine Houser, elderly author. But the truth is, I thought you were just plain *old.*"

"Hey!" She shot him a look that was exactly what he'd aimed for.

He cocked his head to one side and held up a finger. "Ah, but let's talk about my opinion of the mysterious woman at the post office."

"Let's not," she protested. But her smile clearly said the opposite.

"I desperately wanted to get to know her." He hesitated. "Do I dare ask what you were so upset about that day—in the car?"

Madeleine put her spoon down and thought for a minute, then giggled like a schoolgirl.

"What?"

She put an elbow on the table and rested her chin on one hand. "I was upset because my proofreader had just returned my manuscript with a note saying she was quitting."

"Oh. . ." One more piece of the puzzle plunked into place. "Well, hey, didn't you tell me that one day you'd probably be able to laugh about it?"

She laughed again, a sound Art was quickly growing to love.

When her amusement subsided, a wistful note crept into her voice. "I really didn't expect that day to come quite so soon."

"I'm so glad it did."

She rewarded him with another smile. "Me, too."

"Your book is wonderful, Madeleine—may I call you Madeleine?" It felt right, but he wanted to be certain.

"My friends call me Maddie."

He nodded. "Then Maddie it is. And I mean it. Your book is excellent."

"Thank you, Arthur—"

"Please, my friends call me Art."

"Art, then." She bobbed her chin. "I was nervous...about having you read it."

"What? You, nervous about some old geezer's opinion?"

"I'd grown to like that old geezer quite a bit. And to respect his opinion." A mischievous glimmer came to her eyes. "Frankly, I'm not sure how much I'd value the critique of a young whipper-snapper like you."

If he'd believed in love at first sight, he would have dropped to one knee and proposed on the spot. But he managed to restrain himself and simply enjoy her clever wit.

*Maddie.* Yes, the name fit Green Eyes perfectly.

She jumped up and went to the kitchen, came back with a pitcher of water, and refilled his glass.

"Thank you. You don't have to wait on me, you know."

"I don't mind. You're not feeling well. Besides, I can never begin to repay you for allowing me to take over your house like this."

"Speaking of which..." He balled up his napkin and pushed back his chair, "I need to let you get back to work." He gathered up their bowls and spoons and carried them into the kitchen. Poking his head back into the dining room, he added, "Pretend I'm not here. I'll take care of these dishes. You get back to that story. I'm ready for more chapters."

He went back to the kitchen and ran the sink full of hot water. While he washed dishes, he listened to the rhythmic *tap tap tap* of her keyboard. He was wiping off the counters when he heard her giggling again.

He poked his head into the dining room. "Did our story take a humorous turn?"

She looked up and studied him for a moment. "I may as well tell you. You're my hero."

"Wow... Just because I did the dishes?"

"No. The photograph upstairs." She pointed toward the ceiling.

He waited, dish towel in hand.

"Would you care to clue me in? Or would you rather write me a note?" He grinned.

She gave him a crooked smile and dipped her head. "I saw the photograph upstairs of you and your wife. The old-fashioned one. I thought it was you when you were young––before I knew you weren't old, I mean—" She shook her head. "This is very complicated."

He waited, rather enjoying her discomfort.

"I needed a face for my hero and. . .well, I borrowed yours. I hope you don't mind."

Art curbed a grin. "No wonder I liked Jonathan Barlowe so well."

Maddie laughed again and turned a luscious shade of pink. But he was flattered at the implication.

"Ginny said your wife––Annabeth––died." It was almost a whisper.

His breath caught at the sound of Annie's name, but the sympathy in Maddie's expression touched a place deep within. "Yes." He looked at the floor. "Cancer. It'll be three years next April."

"I'm so sorry. She was very beautiful."

He nodded, unable to speak. Suddenly desperate to change the subject, he moved toward the stairway. "I'm keeping you from your work..."

"Oh no." She scooted her chair back from the table. "I'm not going to kick you out of your own dining room. I'll go now. I can come back after you've returned to work."

"Please. Don't go, Maddie. I needed to get busy anyway. I have papers to grade downstairs."

"Well...if you're sure. . ."

"Positive. It was very nice to finally meet you." He smiled and stretched out a hand again. "Madeleine."

She took it, and the pink in her cheeks blossomed. "You, too. . .Arthur."

Downstairs he retrieved a stack of freshman essays from his briefcase and took them to the bar in the kitchen. But thoughts of Annie––and of the woman upstairs––wouldn't let him concentrate.

More than once, the music of feminine laughter floated down the stairway. He didn't know if Green Eyes was writing a funny scene, or if she was, like him, remembering some little incident, some little providential twist of timing that had led to their meeting today.

All he knew was that this house had been too long without a woman's laughter.

Eleven

T he next morning when Maddie emerged from the steamy bathroom, hair still damp from her shower, the answering machine blinked at her. She listened to the message while she did her makeup.

"Hello, Maddie. It's Art. Just wanted to let you know Ginny's soup worked its magic and I'm going back to work today, so the house is all yours. Please make yourself at home. I–I've left you a note. . .in the usual place. Well. . .that's all. Bye now."

A twinge of guilt accompanied the thrill that went up her spine at the sound of Art's voice. But she detected a note of hesitancy, too, and wondered what it meant. She'd dreamed of Arthur Tyler—Art—both waking and sleeping, since she'd left the inn yesterday. She had fallen and fallen hard.

But how could that be? She didn't even know the man. Was she just in love with the idea of being in love?

She stared in the mirror as she ran a brush through her hair. "You don't know what love is, Houser." But oh, how she wanted to learn.

Sitting across from Art over chicken noodle soup yesterday, talking, laughing together, it seemed as though they were dear, old friends. She smiled at her reflection. *Old.* And she did know something of Art's dreams and desires. In a way, they'd been courting since the second day she went to the inn and found his thoughtful note in reply to hers. They just hadn't realized it.

Maddie wondered what he was feeling this morning. Had he sensed the connection as strongly as she? Even though his wife had been gone for several years, it was obvious from his reaction yesterday that he was still reeling from the loss. She'd need to tread lightly.

With a swarm of butterflies in her stomach, she drove out to the inn, feeling a new kind of anticipation over the note that awaited. She let herself in and hurried to the dining room. Without bothering to set up her computer, she picked up the sheet of paper on the table.

As she read, her heart dipped and soared and dipped again like a kite in a fickle Kansas wind.

*Dear Maddie,*

*Not Ms. Houser, not Madeleine, but dear Maddie. I'm still trying to sort out all the crazy misunderstandings that kept us from meeting until yesterday. But somehow I know it was for the best. I think perhaps if we'd met that first day you came to write at the inn, we never would have grown to know and respect one another as we have. (At least I hope you share those feelings.)*

*I suppose you need to know that I've put up some walls where women—especially beautiful, talented, available women—are concerned. My marriage was an extremely happy one, but it had a tragic ending. And since you and I have been honest with each other from the start, I'll confess to a tremendous fear that I will never be able to love that way again. I don't want you to expect what I'm not sure I can give.*

*Perhaps I am seriously premature in sharing these things with you—and now in making a request—but what I said yesterday was true: I would like to get to know you better. Could we have dinner again soon? A real—dare I say it—date? If I've misread your inter-*

*est, please be honest with me, and please forgive me. But if not, are you free this Saturday night? The college symphony is performing, and I have two tickets. (And someone told me about a new restaurant not far from campus. We could eat before the concert.)*

*I admit I'm a little nervous about this next step in our friendship. Frankly I adored the elderly, charming, safe Madeleine Houser. I'm a little sad to think she's gone from my life. But I have a feeling her younger counterpart will win me over just as quickly. In fact, I'm not so sure she hasn't already.*

*I'll hope to find your response when I get home tonight, but if you need to think it over for a few days, I will understand.*

*Your friend,*
*Art*

Maddie read the note again, caressing the smooth paper beneath her palm. How was she supposed to finish her novel, make her deadline, *breathe,* when his letter contained such undisguised hesitancy—such fragile promise?

She read it a third time and found herself more confused than ever. What did the man want? First it seemed as if he were making romantic overtures, but then he held out a warning that no one could fill Annie's place in his heart. Yet in his very next breath he was asking her for a date. Did the man have a clue what he wanted? Did he care that he was stringing her along like some kind of puppet?

She picked up her pen and turned over Art's note, ready to write her reply on the back. But she didn't want to part with this paper. She needed to take it home and read it again, attempt to decipher the true message his words held.

Digging in her computer bag, she found a legal pad. She sat for several minutes, pen poised, mind reeling, before she knew what she wanted to say.

. . .

*Dear Art,*

*Rest assured, I am every bit as frightened and uncertain as you are. Having said that, my calendar is free for Saturday, and I can't think of a more pleasant way to spend it than at dinner and the symphony with a friend.*

*Shall we keep it at that, with no other expectations or potential? Just friends? I could use a friend right now.*

*Maddie*

She laid the pen and pad on the table. She understood what Art meant about being sad to see the imagined, elderly friend go. She felt the same about "old Mr. Tyler." With him, she'd never had to measure her words so carefully. Never had to worry that she would be judged the way men her age judged women.

Had they ruined a wonderful friendship by the simple act of being introduced? Did the mere fact that they were the same age, and therefore eligible for romance, doom their friendship? This surely broke her track record for destroying a relationship. Friends to strangers almost before she met the guy.

She opened her laptop, pulled up her manuscript, and forced herself to start typing. But what she really wanted was to put her head in her hands and weep.

On Thursday evening Art sat in Ginny Ross's cozy living room, sipping tea from a fragile china cup. They'd discussed global news and local politics, and now they'd worked their way down to the weather.

Beside him on the slipcovered sofa, Ginny set her own teacup on the doily-strewn coffee table. "Well, enough small talk. What did you really come for, Arthur?"

Art smiled. Ginny had never been one to mince words. Okay, he would lay it all out for her and see if she had a cure for his jumbled emotions. "I think I'm in love with your neighbor."

Ginny hooked a thumb to the north and feigned shock. "Elma Wheaton? I don't know, Art. She's awfully old for you, don't you think?"

"Very funny, Ginny. You know exactly who I mean." He sobered. "I think I'm in love with Madeleine Houser."

Ginny's expression was unreadable. "So why are you telling *me?* Seems Madeleine ought to be the first to hear this startling announcement."

"She already has. . .well, sort of."

"Arthur, how do you 'sort of' tell a woman you love her? Seems to me either you do or you don't."

"Ginny—"

Her eyes softened, and she reached over to pat his knee. "It's Annie, isn't it?"

"I know it's not right to hold on, Ginny. I know it, but I don't know what to do about it."

"Art, Annie's not coming back. Ever. I know you understand that," she said gently. "And I know Annie wanted you to go on with your life."

He swallowed hard. "I'm just. . .so afraid that no one will ever be able to compare to her. We had such a good thing, Ginny. Right up until the end—a *perfect* thing and—"

"No, it *wasn't* perfect, Art." Ginny wagged her head. "My memory sometimes tends to gloss over the bad times Grover and I had, too. But that wouldn't be right. It wouldn't be honest. Oh, it was *mostly* good, just as it was for you and Annie. But don't forget the struggles, Art. Don't romanticize things. That's not fair—not to Annie, and certainly not to Madeleine."

Art thought about Ginny's words. Yes, he and Annie had sometimes fought. But they'd never let the sun go down on their anger. They'd never hurt each other beyond forgiveness. It was nothing he could take credit for. It was all Annie. Her spirit had been ever gentle and loving, even after she'd become so ill.

"What if. . .what if I marry someone else and it's not as good as it was with Annie? I've known what marriage can be. I can't risk ruining the memories I have with Annie."

Ginny leaned in and took both his hands in hers. Her frail, veined hands were dwarfed by his own, but there was surprising strength in her grasp.

"Arthur Tyler..." She gave his hands a little shake that made him look her in the eye. "I know you well enough to know that you, of all people, are not going to do anything to sully the institution of marriage. Unless you're putting your faith in yourself. But I know you better than that. You've always been one to trust God for your life. Why are you withholding this one thing now?"

"I–I guess I didn't realize I was."

"Well, you are."

He didn't reply. Didn't need to.

Art looped one end of his necktie over the other and tied the knot unconsciously. The man staring back at him from the mirror certainly didn't *look* riddled with guilt. He wished they could trade places.

It was wrong to feel this way. He knew that. Annie had been gone a long time. And Ginny was right: Annie had given her blessing for him to find love again. At the time, he'd resented it, still refusing to believe God would ever take his Annie from him. For a long time after she died, her blessing was meaningless, since he'd had no desire to even look at another woman.

But now there was a living, breathing woman who had stolen into his life under cover of acute misunderstanding, and he'd fallen in love almost without realizing it. Okay, maybe it was a stretch to call it love. He didn't really know Maddie. Yet he felt he did. The notes they'd shared had opened windows into each of their hearts. Reading her manuscript had opened a door. And now having met her, having discovered that they shared much more than he'd ever imagined, he could not deny she made his heart pump to a rhythm he'd long forgotten.

Wednesday he'd sat across the table from a beautiful woman, and for the first time since Annabeth McGee, he'd experienced that enthralling pull on his heartstrings. It had energized him like nothing had in a very long time.

Three days later, that tug on his heart had become a tug-of-war. And right now, guilt was pulling far more weight on the rope of his emotions. Luckily, Maddie didn't appear to be as smitten as he was. In truth, his heart had sunk when he read her rather cool note. She seemed determined to remain friends and nothing more. But perhaps that was a good thing.

Then there was the matter of their date. No, he mentally corrected himself. If she only wanted to be friends, he had to quit thinking of tonight as a date. Maddie was probably dressing for the evening this very minute. He wondered how she would look all dressed up.

*Stop it, Tyler. She's a friend. That's all.* An image of her pale, wavy hair and those tantalizing green eyes popped into his mind. He could almost hear the melody of her laughter. His thoughts were hardly appropriate toward a woman who was only a friend. But he couldn't help it.

He was going to drive himself insane thinking this way. With a sharp tug, he finished his tie, patted his pockets to be sure the symphony tickets were there, and headed out to the pickup.

Twelve

**M**addie paced the living room, making occasional forays into the bathroom to check her lipstick, add one last spritz of hairspray, and adjust the collar of her white silk blouse.

It wasn't often she got to dress up, and it had been rather fun to go all out this evening. She just hoped she hadn't overdone it. She didn't want Art to get the wrong idea.

The front doorbell chimed. Maddie's breath caught in her throat. She slipped on a cashmere sweater, rubbed damp palms on her long velvet skirt, and went to answer the door.

Art stood on the porch, handsome in a dark suit with a tie the same shade of blue as his eyes. "Maddie. You. . .look lovely."

She felt certain, looking into the deep pools of those eyes, that it wasn't the appreciation of a mere friend she saw there. "You clean up pretty nice, too," she teased, determined to keep things light.

Art led the way down the front walk. November had come in on a crisp breeze and she shivered and pulled her sweater tighter. Art went around to open the door for her. It was a bit of a climb to get into his pickup, but she managed to do so without looking like a total klutz. He carefully tucked the hem of her skirt out of harm's way before closing the door.

They were silent while Art navigated the tree-lined streets to the edge of town. He merged easily into the flow of traffic on the interstate and set the cruise control. "This symphony is probably going to seem pretty Podunk to you—compared to the concerts you hear in New York, I mean."

She waved off his warning. "It's been so long since I've been to a real concert, I doubt I'd know one from a kindergarten kazoo band."

He laughed. "That's good, because that may be exactly what this group sounds like to your ears."

"Art, I do love classical music, but I'm no critic."

"Well, we'll see after tonight." He flashed a droll grin.

For the rest of the drive into Wichita, they talked animatedly about music and movies and books they'd enjoyed. In the space of an hour, she successfully eliminated her earlier image of Art as a distinguished, elderly professor and replaced it with the witty, handsome, flesh-and-blood man seated behind the wheel of this Chevy 4x4––an exchange she made gladly.

Art asked about her writing career and gave a glowing critique of her work-in-progress. "I'm not finished yet," he said, "but what I've read so far is beautifully done. I will truly feel guilty if you pay me to proofread this, Maddie."

"Well, if you won't let me pay you, then you'd better quit reading right now, because I'm already so indebted to you for the use of the inn, I'll never get out of hock."

"Hey," he said lightly, "can we come to some sort of under-standing about this? We both feel we're cheating the other, so let's just call it even and not bring it up again."

She nodded. "I could go with that plan."

They ate at a new Italian place on the east side of town. Dinner brought more pleasant conversation. Again, Maddie had the sense she'd known this man forever.

Later, in spite of Art's caveat, Maddie thoroughly enjoyed the concert. The small symphony was quite accomplished, and several of Maddie's favorite concertos were on the program. She was sorry when it was over. On the way out the door, Art purchased one of the group's CDs, and they listened to it on the drive home.

"You know," she said, as strains of Mendelssohn threaded around them, "when I saw this pickup truck, I was just sure we'd be listening to country music all the way."

Art smiled. "I like to keep people guessing."

*Boy, did he have* that *right.*

"Actually, I do listen to country," he said. "I like the stories those ballads tell. But there's something timeless about the classics."

"Did your wife. . .did Annie like classical music?" Maddie ventured, wanting to be sure he knew the topic wasn't off-limits for her.

There was an overlong silence.

Maddie remembered Art's quick exit the last time the topic of Annabeth came up, and for a minute she was afraid she'd stepped on sacred ground.

"Yes, she did like music," Art said finally. "Annie played the piano beautifully and always had Mozart or Vivaldi going on the stereo. She always wanted to get a piano, but once we opened the inn there just wasn't the space." He rested one wrist on the steering wheel. "Do you play? Piano?"

She cringed and shook her head. "Only for my own enjoyment. I play by ear––by heart, my mom calls it."

"I'm sure you play beautifully."

"Oh, I would never inflict my pathetic attempts on an audience. But it's cheap therapy. I'm out of practice, though. My sister's piano is desperately out of tune, and I left my piano in storage in New York."

"Are you going back?" he asked abruptly. "To New York, I mean? Is Clayburn only temporary?"

She wondered how much rode on her answer. "I honestly don't know. My mom is only sixty-eight. She could live for many years. I want to be here for her."

"How is she doing?"

Maddie was moved by the genuine concern in his voice. "That's a hard question to answer. I don't think she's known me for quite a while now."

"That must be really difficult for you. I admire you. . .for wanting to be there for her."

She shook her head. "I'm not doing anything heroic. But I am glad it's worked out for me to be here. And I do like Clayburn. More than I thought I would." She didn't tell him that *he* was a lot of the reason why. "If it weren't for the house being so torn up, I couldn't complain."

"Oh, but if it weren't for the house being torn up, you wouldn't be sitting here beside me right now. I tend to think that was a gift."

His words confused her as much as his note had. This had to stop. She drew herself up in the seat. "Art, I—I'm too old to play games, so I want to get this out in the open."

"Okay. . ." His tone was understandably cautious.

She took a deep breath. "Your note the other day confused the life out of me."

He seemed surprised. "What do you mean?"

"In one breath you're asking me for a date, and in the next you're warning me you've put up this wall because of Annie. Then you change gears again and say I've already won you over— whatever that means." Against her will, her voice went up an octave. "And now you're saying our friendship is a gift. At least I think that's what you meant. The thing is, I don't have a clue where I stand with you. I don't know if you're determined we can never be more than friends or if you truly meant this night to be. . .a date." She felt a little foolish—and more than a little vulnerable after laying everything out so blatantly.

Art raked a hand through his hair, then put both hands back on the steering wheel and stared straight ahead for a long minute. She was afraid she'd ticked him off.

When he finally spoke, his voice was so quiet she could scarcely hear it over the truck's engine. "Maddie... I'm sorry."

He reached across the seat and took her hand in his. A tiny tremor went up her spine.

His Adam's apple bobbed in his throat. "If I've confused you, it's only because I'm confused myself. I–I do want to get to know you. No. . ." He turned to meet her gaze briefly before training his eyes back on the road. "As long as we're being totally honest here, the truth is, I feel as though I *do* know you. And I–I like what I see, Maddie. I like it a lot. I don't just mean what I see with my eyes, although that's altogether pleasant, too."

For a moment, his eyes sought hers again, and he gave her hand a squeeze. Maddie felt the pleasure of his words warm her cheeks.

"What I really mean is. . .well––" His grin turned impish. "I had a bit of a crush on you when I thought you were eighty years old. But you were *safe* then. You weren't going to mess up the comfortable little world of grief I've lived in...gotten comfortable in, as dumb as that might sound." He waited, as though wanting a response.

But she didn't know what to say.

"I know this sounds totally unreasonable, Maddie, but now that I've met you, I feel like I'm almost. . .I don't know. . .in love with you—which would be wonderful if that feeling weren't eating me alive with guilt."

What? She stared at him. Now he was in *love* with her? The man was crazy––and driving her there on a fast train. She finally found her voice. "You feel guilty because of Annie?"

He nodded, but even in the darkness of the truck's cab, he couldn't hide the emotion that tinted his expression.

"Art. . ." She pulled her hand out of his warm grasp. "I've had my heart broken enough times that I don't go seeking out the experience. There's no way I can compete with. . .with a memory. And if you're looking for someone to ease your guilt, I'm sorry, but I don't think I'm your gal."

"I'm sorry," he said. "I want to be able to open my heart again. I truly do. And I've never said that to any woman before. But. . .I can't seem to find the way."

She stared at her lap. "Thank you for being honest with me. I think."

"I'm trying, Maddie, that's all I can promise."

"I know. . .I know you are. But I don't know if my heart can take the chance that you'll fail."

They drove the rest of the way home in silence. When they got to her house, Art came around and opened her door. She rummaged frantically in her purse, looking for her keys, not wanting to create an awkward moment at the door.

She finally found them in a corner of her bag. She jangled them in front of her.

"Let me walk you to the door." Art smiled, and she felt her heart respond.

"It's okay. You don't have to."

"Maddie—" He scuffed the toe of his shoe in the gravel. "I don't want to sound like a broken record, but I'm sorry. I've ruined what has been a delightful evening till now."

"It's okay, Art. You can't help what you feel." She made her voice bright. "I enjoyed the concert very much. And thank you for dinner. It was delicious."

She turned and started up the walk. She was aware of his pickup idling in the drive until he saw she was safely in the house. She locked the front door behind her, flipped off the lights, and parted the curtain. She watched him back out of her driveway, and followed the taillights of his truck until they disappeared from sight. Letting the drapes fall, she put a hand over her heart in a futile effort to assuage the ache there.

Art had said he wanted to open his heart again.

Well, she'd done just that, and look where it had gotten her.

She crossed the room to Kate's old upright piano and ran her fingers idly over the dusty keys. Their sour, metallic clang pierced the stillness. A dissonant note hung in the air, and Maddie closed her eyes. She was playing at love the way she played the piano––by heart.

92

*Thirteen*

**B**ack at the inn, Art got ready for bed, but sleep eluded him. Finally he crawled from beneath the covers and paced his apartment into the wee hours of the morning, thinking, praying, agonizing. The pain he'd seen in Maddie's eyes tonight broke his heart. He'd done that to her.

He wanted so desperately to put the past behind him, to offer Maddie his love with no reservations. But what kind of man would he be if he could let Annie go so easily?

On a whim, he went to the closet and pulled their wedding album from the top shelf. He sank to the floor at the foot of the bed and put the album in his lap. He'd nearly worn the pages out those first weeks after she died. But months had passed since he'd last looked at the photographs and mementos tucked inside. As he leafed through the pages, he remembered why. The vivid images made him remember every curve of her face, every nuance of her smile. In one shot, the camera had captured Annie's luminous expression as she walked down the aisle toward him. She'd been oblivious—they both had—to the horror that would ravage their lives a short decade later.

Art turned the last page and slowly eased the cover closed. As he put the album aside on the floor, another book caught his eye.

The hardcover copy of Maddie's novel, the one that had revealed her identity to him. *Hope's Song.* He slid it from the shelf again, flipped open the back cover, and stared at her image. Judging by the book's copyright date, the photograph must have been at least four or five years old. Maddie's hair was shorter and curlier. But her smile was the same. . .and the sparkle of her eyes.

He riffled the pages absently, deep in thought. Something caught his eye. Yellow highlighting and notes scribbled in Annie's handwriting. How often had he scolded her for dog-earing and marking in their books? It had been a source of frustration for him. But her friends loved to borrow her books. It was like getting a free study guide, they always said.

He thought about what Ginny had said that afternoon and remembered a heated argument he'd had with Annie over what he viewed as her careless disrespect of books. He'd called her irresponsible and wasteful. And brought her to tears.

Ginny was right. It hadn't all been a bed of roses. They'd had their ugly moments.

He flipped through the pages and read a few of Annie's cryptic marginal notes. "Echoes the theme of Pastor Rennick's sermon," one read. "Share with study group!" said another.

It was a gift to have this peek into Annie's heart. But his own heart stuttered when he saw his name in the margin. "Read this section to Art."

Had she done so? Annie was always reading him snippets, but he didn't remember her ever reading from Maddie's books. Of course, he hadn't known Maddie then. He read the highlighted paragraphs and scratched his head. What had Annie intended him to glean from the words? Turning to the cover flap, he read the synopsis of the book, trying to put the passage she'd marked into context.

The novel was set during the Civil War. His gut twisted when he read that the heroine was dying of consumption. No wonder Annie identified with the storyline. He read the paragraphs again.

. . .

*Mitzy came in and flung open the window, muttering something about fresh air. A minute later, the servant sashayed out of the room with the washbasin sloshing, leaving the scent of lavender in its wake. Sarah watched from the bed, her thin fingers worrying the rough hem of the coverlet. Mitzy had not so much as glanced her way. Sarah blanched. Had she become invisible in her confinement?*

*Her gaze traveled to the window, and in an instant, she felt transported beyond the splintered sash. Her sick room faded to nothing, and she was somehow dancing among the willows that bent in the April breeze. She could almost feel the cool grasses between her bare toes, relish the warmth of the sun on her arms. For one moment, she remembered what it had been like to be healthy and whole. It was a gift. And even as her spirit danced, she thanked the Giver.*

Had Annie experienced something similar during her illness? Or was there some deeper meaning he wasn't quite getting? He would show the passage to Maddie. Maybe she would understand what Annie might have wanted him to learn from it.

Paging through the last half of the book, he came to a notation on the last page. It was printed in bold letters and underlined twice: "I LOVE this author!"

Stunned, he lifted his eyes to the ceiling––and beyond. *Amazing.* Annie had met Maddie through her words––had connected with her heart, her soul, her faith in God––and had come to love her. Perhaps *this* was the message he most needed to hear right now. The sign he'd been looking for.

He turned to the author's photograph again and brought it slowly to his lips. He was finally ready to let go. And he could hardly wait to tell Maddie.

Fourteen

The granite countertops were elegant, and Maddie's good china gleamed behind glass fronted cabinets. She walked across the pristine tiled floor and stood in the doorway surveying the results of weeks of chaos and labor. It was finally finished. And it was beautiful.

Maddie sighed. Her days would finally belong to her again. No more letting in a crew of noisy workmen every morning or tripping over sawhorses at night. No more microwaved suppers. No more hauling her entire office back and forth each day. The house was livable, and she could set up her office and finish her book in peace.

So why did she feel so melancholy?

Stupid question. She knew why.

It had been nearly a week since her disastrous date with Arthur Tyler. Except for the friendly, noncommittal notes on the dining room table, she had not seen him or spoken to him. And today would be her last day at the inn. She would sit at the smooth oak table and listen to the familiar, soothing creaks of the old house. She would write her chapters and coax Alex to warm her feet. She would jot down one last note of thanks to Arthur Tyler. And then she'd come home.

*Home.* The very word filled her with longing. As beautiful as it was, Kate's fancy house with its new kitchen and spacious rooms had never quite felt like home to her. Even the New York loft Maddie loved couldn't hold a candle to the one place that had worked its way into her heart. In the space of a few weeks, Annabeth's Inn had become home to Maddie.

It wasn't the bricks and boards or the cottonwoods and rosebushes—or even the lovable cat—that made it feel like home. It was Art. And knowing that, she wasn't sure she could ever really feel at home again anywhere else.

Sighing again, she went to gather her things. She loaded the car and backed out of the driveway. Today, the short drive to the inn felt like a walk to the gallows. She turned onto Hampton Road and a few minutes later turned the key in Art's front door. She walked through the hall to the dining room. As always, his note was waiting—a short one today. Had he remembered this was her last day?

She set up her computer and started coffee, putting off the moment when she would read Art's final note. When she finally picked it up, his salutation startled her.


*Dearest Maddie,*

*Today is supposed to be your final day at the inn. I know you have a book to finish and I know your deadline is tight, but could I bring lunch at noon and steal a few minutes of your time? There's something I'd like to talk to you about. (If you can't spare the time, I understand. Just leave a message on my cell phone.)*

*Happy writing,*
*Art*

She turned the note over, hoping to find a postscript that would offer a clue. But the page was blank. How did he expect her to concentrate, knowing he'd be walking through the door in a few hours?

She went into the bathroom off the main-floor bedroom and inspected her reflection. Why hadn't she bothered to fix her hair this morning instead of gathering it into a sloppy ponytail? And chosen something besides yoga pants and sweatshirt—although she did like the way the teal color brought out the green flecks in her eyes.

What difference did it make what she wore, how she looked? It didn't matter. None of it mattered.

She barely managed to write a thousand words before the clock struck twelve. Right on schedule, she heard the key in the door to the apartment below. She moistened her lips and quickly put her computer in sleep mode.

Footsteps sounded on the stairway, and Maddie went to meet him. Art balanced two round plastic containers in his hands and was attempting to secure two large paper cups with his chin while the cat wove a figure eight between his feet.

She hurried down the steps. "Here, let me take some of this. Alex, shoo! Mmm. . .smells good. What are we having?"

"Chicken noodle soup." Art grinned and winked at her. "I'm told it's good for what ails you."

Why did he always have to flirt with her? If he didn't have room in his heart for another woman, why did he turn on the charm when he was with her?

She took the soup into the kitchen and transferred it to thick pottery bowls. Enticing aromas filled the room. "Is this from the deli?" she called out to the dining room, where she heard him scooting chairs around. The drinks bore the deli's label, but their takeout usually came in Styrofoam containers.

He came and stood in the doorway between the two rooms and watched while she fixed a tray with crackers and spoons. "The drinks are from the deli. Actually Ginny made the soup."

"Really?" That was interesting. Ginny'd been over the night before to borrow the newspaper. She hadn't mentioned anything about soup.

Maddie swept past Art, carrying the tray to the table. Art put folded napkins at each place and removed lids from their drinks. He came and held her chair for her.

"Thank you, sir."

He took the chair to her left and spread a napkin on his lap. "Shall we bless the food?"

Maddie nodded and bowed her head.

Art surprised her by reaching for her hand. His grasp was warm and firm—and unsettling.

"Father God, we thank You for this day and for this food. Please bless our time together, and especially bless the dear hands that prepared this food. In Jesus' name, amen."

He squeezed Maddie's hand before he let it go.

They ate in silence for a few minutes, then Art wiped his mouth and pushed back from the table. "I want to talk to you about something."

She swallowed a mouthful of soup and put down her spoon. "So you said, in your note."

Art bent his head and rubbed circles in the smooth finish of the table with his fingertips. "I owe you an apology. You. . .well, you took me by surprise that day I first realized who you were. Before I'd had time to think about the consequences, I'd already asked you for a date. That wasn't fair to you."

Maddie's defenses went up. Here it came—the big breakup scene that was all too familiar. Never fear, though. She had her lines memorized.

Meanwhile, Art dutifully delivered his own lines. "The truth is, I was a very confused man. I wasn't looking for another relationship because. . .well, I guess I'd known true love, and I didn't believe I could ever find that with anyone else."

From the edge of her consciousness, Maddie became aware

that Art was speaking in the past tense. She started to pay attention.

"For a while, grief crippled me," he said. "But I've been talking to some very wise counselors recently, and I do believe they've brought me to my senses."

"C–counselors?" She waited.

With one easy motion, he straddled his chair and moved it closer to hers. He enveloped her right hand in both of his. "Maddie, I don't want to rush you, but I don't want to let you get away, either. When you told me your house was finished and that you wouldn't be coming out here to write any more, it. . ." He shook his head and swallowed hard. "It scared me. I know it sounds crazy because it's not like we were ever here together. But I liked coming home to find your notes. Highlight of my days, and I'll miss them like crazy. I liked walking up the stairs and catching the faintest whiff of your perfume. And that day I was home sick. . . Oh, Maddie, you can't imagine how wonderful it was to hear your laughter up here. I don't want to lose that."

Though her backside was firmly planted on the brocade pad of the chair, Maddie felt some part of her rise up and begin to soar.

Alex sauntered to the table, tail held high, and situated himself between them. The cat looked from Maddie to Art and back again, then pushed his weight hard against Maddie's leg, begging to be petted.

"Go away, Alex." Art gave the cat a gentle shove with the side of his foot. "Come on, Buddy. You're cramping my style."

Alex plopped down on top of Maddie's feet. Art ignored him and scooted his chair another inch closer. "What I'm trying to say is, I know now it's very possible I may find love again. And I'm ready to embrace the possibility."

She sat, speechless. One hot tear escaped and rolled down her cheek.

Art let go of her hand. He reached up to thread his fingers

through her hair and smudged the tear away with his thumb. "Oh, Maddie, I'm so sorry if I hurt you. Could we begin again?"

She nodded, her heart as full as her throat.

Art stroked her hair away from her temple and looked into her eyes. "I desperately want to kiss you right now. Would that be okay?"

In an instant, she was in his arms, and then he was kissing her forehead, her temples, his lips brushing away the tears of joy that streaked her cheeks. Finally, gently, he matched his lips to hers.

When he drew away, they were both breathless.

"Wow..." Maddie drew out the word.

"Yeah, wow," he echoed, kissing her again. He brushed a strand of hair from her face, then cupped her cheek in the palm of his hand. "I have so much I want to tell you. God has done some pretty incredible things in my life these past few days."

"Really?"

He nodded. "You may be the writer, but I have some stories of my own to tell."

She reached up and put her hand over his, savoring the warmth of his skin. "I can't wait to hear your stories, Arthur Tyler."

That familiar spark flared in his smoky eyes. "What if I told you that you were the heroine in some of them?"

She flashed him a grin. "I'd say turnabout is fair play."

Their mingled laughter rang through the house.

Fifteen

A rt tamped the snow shovel on the driveway and stepped back to admire his work. The walk was clear, but the porch railings that wrapped around the house wore pristine shawls of snow. They sparkled in the late January sun. Maddie had allowed him to shovel the walk only for the sake of the guests, who'd be arriving within the hour.

But she'd been adamant about leaving the snow on the railings intact. If he remembered correctly, *picturesque* was the word she'd used. And he had to admit, the inn did look nice after the skies had deposited eight inches of the white stuff on its roof and eaves.

With her manuscript barely turned in on time, he'd expected her to be frantic about the wedding plans and logistics of their friends and family who were coming in for the event, but if Art had learned anything about Madeleine Houser––soon to be Maddie Tyler––it was that she didn't let many things rattle her. "God has it all under control," she'd told him before they kissed goodnight on the inn's front porch last night.

The last night they'd spend apart. *Ever*, if he had anything to say about it. He could hardly make it seem real that today was his wedding day. He'd been afraid thoughts of Annie––and a twinge of guilt––might dampen his joy. But he was surprised to discover that although Annie, and the wedding day he'd shared with her, were very much on his mind, he was flooded with peace in the midst of it all. *Thank you, Lord.*

Maddie's sister, Kate, had come earlier in the week and quickly assumed the bossy big sister role. His instructions were to stay out of their way and do whatever Maddie told him in preparation for the wedding. When Art told Pastor Rennick that, the man had nodded knowingly. "Sounds like everything is under control then."

Now the inn was ready inside and out, and he went to get the car. His final duty before donning a tux and assuming his position in front of the fireplace, was to pick up Maddie's mom from the nursing home. He and Maddie had taken her out for a drive in the country a couple of weeks ago, and he'd practiced, with Maddie's help, transferring Mildred Houser from the wheelchair to the car, folding the chair and stowing it in the trunk, then doing it all in reverse.

Half an hour later, with Mrs. Houser seated at the back beside Ginny near the aisle Maddie would walk down, he ran down to his apartment to get dressed. He hadn't seen Alex since breakfast, but no doubt the cat was hiding out from the strangers who'd been coming and going all week getting things ready for the wedding.

Knotting the silver tie Maddie picked out for him, he heard Jed and Kate and the girls upstairs greeting guests. Chairs scraped on the floor overhead and a pleasant murmur of mingled voices floated down to him. He adjusted his cufflinks and checked his watch. Almost time. His nerves ratcheted up a notch. He gave his tie a final tug, slipped into his jacket, and headed upstairs.

Six rows of rented chairs had been arranged facing the fireplace, and from the back of the room he observed the small gathering of friends and family unnoticed. He was surprised how many had come out on a Saturday. A couple of colleagues from the university and their wives visited in hushed voices on the back row, and a knot of friends from church held down the fort on the other side of the aisle.

Dave Sanders, who'd agreed to stand up with him, caught his eye and came to clap him on the shoulder and shake his hand. "Hey, buddy... You ready for this?"

"I'm ready."

Pastor Rennick went to the front and Dave joined him while Art went to get Maddie's mom.

In the corner of the dining room, a string quartet from the college tuned their instruments. The exquisite dissonance seemed a perfect metaphor for this new beginning. The room quieted in anticipation.

Art bent to kiss Ginny's cheek, and the lump that moved into his throat surprised him.

"Break a leg," she said, with a comical pump of her fist.

Chuckling and feeling instantly more at ease, Art patted Mildred Houser's hand and wheeled her to the spot reserved on the aisle at the front row. He kissed her cheek as he had Ginny's and took his place at the front of the room beside Dave.

Kate came from a side door and joined them on the other side of the fireplace as the opening strains of Purcell's "Trumpet Tune" swelled and overflowed the inn.

Ginny rose from her chair and went to stand at the bottom of the stairs. That was the cue for all to rise and face the staircase. The banister was festooned with ivy and baby's breath, and candles glowed from hurricanes tied to each baluster post. The inn had never looked better.

Annie would have been delighted. Art somehow knew that... knew it as surely as his love for Maddie Houser grew with every moment he spent with her. He turned toward the staircase.

This was it. And he'd never been more ready in his life.

Maddie stood at the top of the stairway looking down, her heart––and nerves––aflutter. *Please don't let me fall.*

As soon as that prayer left her heart, another took wing behind it. A simple prayer she welcomed and hoped would never leave her repertoire. "Thank you, God," she whispered. "For… everything."

The string quartet's echoed strains of Purcell's lovely air wafted up the stairs, giving the moment a surreal quality. Maddie took a deep breath and gripped her elegant bouquet of white roses in one hand. She caught her reflection in the ornate mirror on the landing and for once she was pleased with what she saw there. She'd planned to wear a cream-colored suit she'd owned for years, but Kate had found this simple tea-length gown on clearance in a Cincinnati boutique and frantically texted photos to Maddie mere days before she'd flown in for the wedding.

The dress was perfect. Absolutely perfect.

The fitted strapless gown had a bodice of appliqué lace and a matching sheer shrug. The satin skirt had just the right amount of flounce and showed off her satin and lace slippers. Kate had helped her with her hair, pulling up the sides, but leaving the back down the way Art liked it. Her sister had tried to talk her into a frothy veil, but Maddie hated it the instant Kate popped it on her head. They'd settled instead on a fragile wreath of baby's breath tucked at her crown.

Maddie descended the first step. Seeing Ginny waiting for her there, her heart swelled. How dear this woman was to her. She blinked back tears and prayed she wouldn't ruin her mascara.

The slanted ceiling prevented her from seeing more than Art's feet until she was halfway down, but when his eyes came into view, all she saw there was love.

She reached the bottom step and took Ginny's arm, but she only had eyes for this man––this amazing man who stood there waiting for her. She couldn't help the smile that came. Nothing had ever felt so right, so true.

When she reached her mother's wheelchair, she knelt beside it and whispered, "I love you, Mom." Maddie kissed her cheek and stood quickly before the tears came again. Taking Ginny's hand, she squeezed it and stepped up to the altar, Ginny still beside her.

Pastor Rennick greeted the audience and said pleasant words that Maddie barely heard. But when he asked, "Who gives this woman to be married to this man?" Ginny lifted her chin and answered strong and clear, "Her mother and I."

The guests sighed in unison, obviously moved by the moment. Maddie hugged Ginny and waited for her to find her seat beside Mom. Then she turned to her groom.

Art took her hand in his, squeezing her fingers, stroking her palm with his smooth thumb in a silent language meant only for them.

"You look so beautiful," he mouthed, when they'd turned their backs to their guests.

Pastor Rennick let them have a moment, and then he spoke the timeless vows. "Arthur Tyler, do you take this woman...?" And, "Madeleine Houser, do you take this man...?"

*Yes. Oh, yes... I do.*

She repeated the promises, committing to memory the planes of her beloved's face, the glint in his eyes. "I promise to love and cherish you, in sickness and in health, for richer or for poorer, and forsaking all others as long as we both shall live."

They exchanged rings and the pastor smiled as he addressed them before the congregation. "Therefore, by the power vested in me, I now pronounce you husband and wife. You may kiss your——"

*Meow.*

Muffled gasps rose from the audience and Dave Sanders's children laughed out loud. In unison, Art and Maddie looked down to see Alex winding figure eights between their legs, tail fluffed and held high.

Maddie stifled a giggle.

Art winked at her and reached to scoop up the cat with one arm. He placed Alex ceremoniously in the surprised pastor's arms.

Then he turned and took Maddie into his arms and kissed her long and sweet.

The guests rose, clapping and cheering, and the string quartet burst into a joyous rendition of Mendelssohn's Wedding March.

Art slid his hand down her arm and grasped her hand again, entwining her fingers with his. Together, they turned to face their loved ones for the first time as husband and wife.

Maddie practically floated down the aisle beside him.

A new year, a new life, a new beginning.

Deborah Raney

Raney Day Press

*One*

M*adeleine Houser Tyler*. Maddie signed her name—her full married name—on the digital contract and looked up from her laptop screen at Art, unable to contain the smile that came. "Shall I hit send?"

Her husband's handsome face held an inscrutable expression.

"What?" She scooted her chair away from the dining room table and turned to face him full-on. "Are you having second thoughts, honey?" The endearment was still new enough to thrill her every time it rolled off her tongue.

Art shook his head as if coming out of a deep reverie. "No. No, of course not. Just...thinking."

"About what? You don't seem very excited." Of course, why would he? It was *her* contract. For three books set in Paris. A brand-new series with a publisher who seemed committed to taking her to the next level with her career. And in her husband's defense, the tight deadlines she'd agreed to would take extended hours at her desk.

"I'm sorry, love. I didn't mean to put a damper on your big moment." He leaned to kiss her cheek. "I'm thrilled for you. Truly, I am."

"But…?"

"No buts. No ifs, ands, *or* buts. I couldn't be happier for you." He rose and came around behind her, massaging her neck and shoulders.

"*Mmm*. That feels good. I'll remember your massage therapy talents when I've been hunched over my computer for hours on end this spring."

His fingers stilled. "Did you forget that I'll be teaching while you're home writing?"

"I know, I know. I'm just teasing. As agreed, I'll have a hot seven-course dinner waiting for you every night at six sharp."

"Three courses will probably suffice. And a hot breakfast for any guests we have staying, right?"

"Except in the summer when *you* take over the cooking. As we agreed."

He grinned. "That sounds fair. As long as I don't have to clean toilets."

She groaned at his not-that-funny joke, but she felt she'd diffused a rehash of an argument they'd had too many times during their fledgling marriage. Six weeks to be exact. Was it normal for newlyweds to average two-point-four arguments per week? About the same topic?

"So? Sign it." Art pointed at her computer screen.

"Wait, let me get my phone and you can take a picture of me signing." She rolled her eyes. "Janice is pushing me to be more active on social media and this would make a good post."

She retrieved her phone from her purse and handed it to him, then struck a pose seated with her hands on the keyboard of her laptop.

He stepped close and held the camera even closer. "Smile."

She leaned away. "Don't get *too* close. I don't want anyone to zoom in and see the details of the contract."

"You can blur it if it shows anything it shouldn't."

He readied the camera again and clicked just as Alex jumped

into her lap, swiping his fluffy tail across her face. She sputtered and picked cat hair off her tongue. "Alex, shoo!"

"Let him stay. Your readers will love it."

She stroked the cat's head, loving the purr it elicited. "You don't think it'll make me look like a crazy cat lady?"

"Well, since you *are* a crazy cat lady now..."

In reply, she hammed a goofy grin, and heard her phone's camera clicking. "Wait. No, I wasn't ready, Art! Take another one."

"Last chance."

She repositioned Alex in her lap and gave Art her best smile.

He clicked several times in succession before handing the phone back to her. "There you go. Now, I need to go mow the lawn before it gets dark."

"Hang on a sec." She held up a hand. "Let me be sure there's something I can use here." She scrolled through the photos he'd just taken. They weren't great, but they'd do. And Alex did look cute. Art was right. Her readers would love it.

He went to the back door and pulled his work jacket from a hook. "Hey, don't forget we have that faculty gathering tomorrow night."

"It's on my calendar. But what should I wear?"

He shook his head. "How would I know?"

"Well, what do the other women wear to these things?"

"Seriously, love? You surely know me well enough by now to know that I pay no attention to fashion trends."

"Can you at least get me in the ballpark? Sparkly formal, Sunday best, or jeans and T-shirt?"

He thought a minute. "Definitely not sparkly formal. Definitely not jeans and T-shirt."

"Okay. Something in between then."

"That sounds right." He slipped on his jacket and disappeared out the door.

"You are no help, professor," she muttered under her breath.

Art parked the car behind half a dozen others on the two-lane, run-of-the-mill street in Wichita's College Hill neighborhood. But the homes on this block in the heart of the city were anything but run-of-the-mill. One glimpse of the president's mansion, and Maddie knew she'd *way* underdressed for this evening. Why hadn't she followed her intuition and thrown some pearls in her purse?

Art jumped out and went around to open her door. As she slid from the passenger seat, he motioned to her jacket folded on the console. "Aren't you going to wear your coat? We might be on the patio part of the evening. And it'll be cold by the time we leave."

"I'm fine. That coat isn't very dressy. In fact it's shabby."

"It's not shabby. And it doesn't have to be dressy to keep you warm."

"I'm fine," she said again, suddenly wishing she were anywhere but here. And suddenly more than a little irked at her husband, who hadn't thought to mention that this gathering was in a three-story brick mansion that had to be at least seven thousand square feet.

Lights twinkled in the landscaping and every window of the house was aglow. A wrought-iron fence offered a sneak peek into a backyard paradise with party lights strung beneath an oversized pergola.

She looked over her shoulder at her husband. "Maybe you should set your sights on becoming president."

Art laughed. "I'm guessing it's not Betsy's salary that paid for this house. Her husband is a surgeon."

"Oh." She shivered as they made their way up a wide flagstone walk that culminated in an imposing arched entry guarded by a decorative gate. "Have you been here before?"

"A couple of times. You'll like the way she decorates."

She doubted it. The home's brick exterior was beautiful, but she was all about cozy. How could a place this massive ever be cozy? She also doubted the president decorated her own home. They'd probably paid thousands to hire a decorator.

The gate swung open moments before they reached it, and a middle-aged woman in a chef's toque and white apron waved them in. "Welcome. I'm just the caterer, but go on through. Everyone's out back. Just follow the noise." The woman hurried around the side of the house and opened the back of an SUV.

Maddie and Art exchanged looks but made their way inside and through an entry hall twice the size of their own living room, then on to a cavernous great room that boasted a fireplace taller than Art. And she did *not* like the decor. Everything—from the offbeat art on the walls to the eclectic mix of sculptures and ornate vases—seemed to serve one purpose: impress.

Entering the kitchen, she could see through open doors to a covered patio in back. Though local nurseries had barely begun to put out their spring annuals yet, the patio was dotted with over-sized stone pots overflowing with pansies and a spring-green vine she didn't recognize.

Guests clustered in small groups, each chattering louder than the one beside it. Watching them, Maddie deflated. The men, like Art, wore suit jackets and white shirts sans ties, but it quickly became clear that among the women, the little black dress was de rigueur for the evening. She looked down at the gray dress slacks she'd spent twenty minutes steaming and the soft cream-colored cable-knit sweater she'd splurged on with her last royalty check and wanted to cry.

Feeling uncharacteristically insecure, she latched onto Art's elbow and pasted on a smile. This was a First World problem of the highest degree. She remembered something Ginny had said the last time they'd had coffee: "Nobody cares how you look if you make *them* feel like a million bucks." That would be her goal tonight. Never mind that their hostess—who was sashaying in their direction right now—was probably already worth *several* million.

"Art! Welcome!" The college president turned her overly whitened smile on Maddie. "And this must be your bride. Welcome, Mrs. Tyler, and congratulations."

"Thank you. And please, call me Maddie. Thank you so much for having us. Your home is lovely." *The exterior anyway*, she corrected, to herself—just so it wouldn't be a lie.

"It's an aging grande dame"—she said it with a bad French accent—"but Frank and I love it."

"I haven't seen Frank yet tonight," Art said.

The woman huffed. "Sadly, he got called in for an emergency surgery this afternoon, but he should be home before long. Now please, help yourself to drinks at the bar. Hors d'oeuvres will be out in a few minutes." With that, President Farroday was off to greet another newly arrived guest.

Art turned to Maddie. "Do you want something to drink?"

"Maybe later."

"Okay. Oh—I see Milton and his wife." He waved back at a man who was beckoning him over. "Come on... I'll introduce you."

She clutched his elbow tighter and followed him across the patio. Art had once shared office space with Milton when they were post-grad teaching assistants, and the two sometimes golfed together but she'd never met him.

One introduction led to another, and as they "worked the room," everyone was welcoming and friendly. Maybe a little too much so. Maddie had the distinct feeling she was being compared and measured against Annabeth—and maybe coming up wanting.

The food was served and they filled their plates and went to stand at a high-top table, visiting with other faculty members and staff and their spouses. Maddie mostly smiled and nodded, and when a couple left their table, she excused herself to find the restroom. Maybe she could kill twenty minutes in there and by the time she found Art again it would be time to go home.

She found the restroom and took her time reapplying lipstick and fixing her mascara. Walking back through the house, she plotted how she might arrange to be "sick" when the next faculty gathering rolled around.

Back on the patio, she spotted Art visiting with two couples she hadn't yet met—fashionably late arrivals maybe? A younger, bearded man held court, seemingly in the middle of a story. Not wanting to interrupt, Maddie slid onto a stone bench behind a newly budded hedge to wait for a lull in the conversation. The sun had set and it would have been chilly but for the radiant patio heaters posted at intervals throughout the yard.

She caught snatches of the conversation on the other side of the bushes, feeling a bit guilty for eavesdropping, but she enjoyed seeing this new-to-her side of Art. It was obvious her husband was well-liked, even admired, by his colleagues, and he seemed confident in his place among them.

When the bearded guy finished his story, someone else piped up. "Has anyone read the new biography of McCullough?"

Maddie leaned in, captured by the question, and wished she'd joined the group before their conversation turned to books. She scooted over on the bench so she could see them through the branches.

"I read it a couple of months ago. It was absorbing only because the man led an interesting life. I doubt *he* would have been impressed with the writing. Pretty sophomoric."

"McCullough will be missed, that's for sure." Art shook his head. "They just don't make writers like that anymore."

"No kidding. The latest *New York Times* bestseller list is a disgrace." The bearded man scoffed. "It's no wonder I have grad students citing sappy YA novels and pop fiction as their literary influence."

"Literary laziness." This from a graying professor who sucked on an unlit pipe. "Popular fiction ought to be outlawed if you ask me."

"Surely you're not advocating banning books, professor?" Art winked at the older man.

"Heavens, no," a female prof quipped. "Then what would we use for toilet paper when the apocalypse comes?"

"You make a good point," the bearded bard conceded to laughter. "I guess there will always be an august purpose to drivel."

The whole lot of them barked like a bunch of seals at feeding time.

Maddie gripped the edge of the concrete bench, feeling the heat rise to her cheeks. Did Art's colleagues know what she did for a living?

And Art was laughing along with them! Though she noticed he glanced around nervously as if he feared she might walk in on their little bashing session.

She had half a mind to charge through the bushes and call them all out. If they had such a low view of popular fiction, didn't that of necessity mean they *read* the stuff? And if they didn't, then how dare they judge it?

They were just jealous that their stuffy literary tomes sat molding in cardboard boxes in their basements while she and her fellow drivel writers laughed all the way to the bank. She gave a little growl of frustration, then clapped a hand over her mouth, afraid she'd given away her hiding place.

But no one turned her way and to his credit, Art did change the subject, asking one of the profs about a new class she was teaching.

Still, Maddie couldn't deny that it stung to realize that her groom had not only not come to her defense, but he'd laughed at the derision aimed at her craft—what she viewed as a gift from God, one that had been a blessing to many people if her reader mail was any indication.

After a few minutes, she circled to the other side of the backyard and then approached the group Art was visiting with. Without meeting her gaze, he drew her to his side with a hand at the small of her back. Did he feel guilty about his disloyalty? His demeanor gave no clue, and the discussion was sidetracked by the president with her surgeon husband in tow.

"Sorry to interrupt," she said, "but Frank is home. I know some of you are new this year and I wanted to introduce you." Betsy Farroday patted her husband's cheek as if he were a little boy. "Darling, this is Dr. Becker and his wife—Judy, isn't it?"

The bearded guy's wife nodded and shook Frank Paulsen's hand. "Nice to meet you, Dr. Farroday."

The president held up a hand. "Oh no, my husband is Frank *Paulsen*. Dr. Paulsen. Doctor, as in surgeon."

"I'm so sorry. I shouldn't have assumed." Judy cringed and her husband looked embarrassed for her.

Dr. Paulsen shook Judy's hand and the president waved off the apology. "An honest mistake. She turned to Maddie and said to her husband, "And I don't believe you've met Arthur Tyler's wife?"

As he had with Judy Becker, the surgeon shook Maddie's hand. "I believe we met several years ago, but you probably don't remember. Annabeth, isn't it?"

"Frank!"

"Good to see you, Dr. Paulsen." Art offered his hand while his left arm came around Maddie's shoulder. "This is my new bride, Madeleine Houser Tyler." He lowered his voice. "Annabeth passed away three years ago—of cancer."

The surgeon swore. "My apologies. I probably knew that and just forgot." He shot daggers at his wife as if she should have informed him. "Well, it's very nice to meet you, Ms. Tyler. And congratulations."

Maddie took his hand and offered the warmest smile she could muster, feeling sorry for his obvious discomfort. "Thank you. Very nice to meet you, too."

"Well, come on. There are others to meet." Betsy Farroday herded her husband toward another group of faculty.

To Maddie's relief, a few minutes later, Art offered excuses, and they made as graceful an exit as possible. He held her hand in silence on the walk to the car. And again, she wondered if he realized how deeply the exchange with his colleagues had hurt.

She would be thankful when they were finally on the interstate back to Clayburn with no neon lights reflecting in the tears on her cheeks.

*Two*

A rt watched Maddie surreptitiously as they wove their way through the downtown streets of Wichita. He didn't know whether to mention Dr. Paulsen's mistaking her for Annie or to just pretend it hadn't happened.

Maddie seemed intent on the nighttime scenes outside her window, but it wasn't like her to be so quiet.

"So," he ventured as he merged onto the interstate, "what did you think of the party?"

He'd begun to think she hadn't heard him when she muttered, "It was okay. For not knowing anyone."

"Well, at least now when I talk about President Farroday or Ned Benson, you'll know who I'm talking about.

"Ned was the one with the beard and horn-rimmed glasses?"

"Right."

Silence.

He tried again. "Did you like the house?"

"I liked the yard. And the architecture was beautiful. But the inside seemed a little... I don't know...pretentious, I guess."

"Pretentious? Why?"

"I don't mean to sound judgy, but *I* would never want to live in a house like that. It seemed like everything was intended to impress. You know... Look how well-traveled we are. Look at the expensive art we've collected. It was kind of off-putting."

"Hmm... I don't know Betsy's husband very well, but I honestly don't think *she's* like that. I mean, sure, they've traveled widely, and they have the money to afford those things, but I've never felt like they were just flaunting it."

"I'm sorry. That wasn't fair. I shouldn't have said anything." She turned away again and looked out the passenger-side window.

"No, it's okay. I asked. You're merely giving your impressions. But I wonder if..." He took a deep breath and risked it. "It probably didn't help that Dr. Paulsen mistook you for Annie."

A sniffle came from the seat beside him.

"Maddie? Is everything okay?" He reached over and sought her hand, but she'd wrapped herself in her "shabby" coat, and she didn't seem to notice his offer. "I'm sorry, love. I know he didn't mean anything by it. I'm sure he's as embarrassed as you were."

"I wasn't embarrassed." She turned to him, the words coming out in a hiss. "At least *that* was an honest mistake."

"Wait... I'm confused. Did someone else say something?"

She gave a little huff. "You could say that."

"Maddie, what happened? I'm in the dark here."

The tilt of her head suggested he should know what she was talking about, or worse that he was the guilty party. He wracked his brain and came up empty. "Hey, what happened? Tell me."

Silence, while he concentrated on the road, but in the dim lights of the dashboard, he sensed more than saw the snide expression she wore.

Finally she said, "I overheard a conversation that did not make me feel very welcome."

"What?" His ire rose in defense of his wife. But then an awful thought struck him. Surely she hadn't overheard *that* conversation. She'd been inside in search of the restroom. He scrambled to remember exactly what had been said, then risked playing dumb. "What did you hear?" But it felt like a lie. And he wasn't a liar.

"What did I hear?" she parroted. In all the months he'd

known her, he'd never heard his wife use such a caustic tone. "Oh, I heard *plenty*. But at least they solved one problem."

"Who? What problem?" He had a sneaking suspicion he was taking some well-placed bait, but like a fool, he went for it anyway. "What's that?"

"Seems they've discovered a great replacement for toilet paper —you know, for when the apocalypse is ushered in."

"Apocalypse?" His breath caught. *He* was caught. *Oh, Lord... help me navigate this one.* "So...you heard that conversation, huh?"

"Every word."

"Maddie, I was not in on that conversation." He sought to temper the defensiveness in his tone. "Except for calling Milt out for advocating book banning, I did not say one word."

"Exactly." He couldn't see her face in the darkness, but he could feel the tension as if it were a third person in the vehicle with them. "You didn't say one word in my defense, Art. In fact, you...you *laughed*!" Her voice broke.

"Maddie. Come on." He put a hand awkwardly on her shoulder since her hands were still locked in the Fort Knox of her jacket. "I didn't mean anything by it. They were just joking around. It was stupid office talk."

"So that's what your days at the office consist of? Bashing the work I'm doing back home? You know, just because I don't write academic, hoity-toity books with six-syllable words or go to an office on an elite campus doesn't mean my work is any less significant than what you do."

"I never said it was." He knew he sounded defensive but she was being ridiculous. "And you know that, Maddie. Come on. I can't help that I was in that circle when the conversation turned sour. But except to call Milt out—and that was in *your* defense—I had nothing to do with the *bashing*." He cringed when the word came out in a mocking tone.

"But you didn't stand up for me either."

"It wasn't even *you* they were talking about. They were talking about popular fiction."

She threw him a look. "Oh, so now my books don't even rise to *popular*?"

He couldn't help it. He laughed. "That's not what I meant."

Another look. Another huff.

They passed the sign for Clayburn's lone exit, and he slowed the car and took the ramp before turning onto Hampton Road. They had guests in two rooms at the inn tonight, so he hoped they could wrap up this discussion before they pulled into the—

"And another thing," she said.

So much for *that* hope. "Hey"—he put a hand on her arm— "do you want to go into town and drive through for coffee?"

"Are you changing the subject?"

"No. Definitely not. Just thought we could get some coffee and drive around and talk things out."

She nodded. "Okay. Sure."

Maddie took the cup from Art at the drive-through and couldn't deny that her husband looked like he'd lost his last friend.

She sighed. She hadn't meant to turn this into an official argument, but she didn't think he realized how much it hurt to have overheard that conversation among his peers. And that he'd laughed at her expense!

He put his own coffee in the cupholder and paid the girl. "Keep the change." The driver of the car behind them tooted his horn impatiently. Art pulled forward to give them access to the window, but he stopped again and asked Maddie, "Is your drink right?"

She took a sip and nodded. "It's fine." In truth, the mocha she'd ordered was lukewarm, but this wasn't the time to complain.

As he pulled onto the street and headed down Clayburn's

main drag, the silence grew between them. She knew she was being petty, but she couldn't seem to get past the empty feeling in the pit of her stomach.

After a few minutes, he turned to her, reaching for her hand across the console. His fingers were warm and the way he entwined them with hers began to melt her. "I'm sorry, Maddie. I shouldn't have laughed. And I should have defended you. Will you forgive me?"

"Of course I forgive you…"

"But…?"

"What do you mean?"

"That didn't sound like wholehearted forgiveness. I heard a 'but' in your voice."

"I do forgive you, but it's not like it was just a little accident." She disentangled her fingers from his. "Your true feelings about the value of my writing—what I see as a *calling*—came through loud and clear when you laughed along with your colleagues while they bashed my work."

"Again, Maddie, they weren't bashing *your* work. They were—"

"And again, Art—" She inhaled, trying to control her mounting anger. "They were bashing the *kind* of writing I do. And you *laughed* along with them!" Her voice broke again, the pain as fresh as if she were back at that stupid faculty gathering hearing the conversation for the first time.

He bored a hole in the windshield with his gaze. But when they reached the edge of town, he pulled over at the entrance to a farmer's field and put the car in Park. He angled his body toward her, resting his left arm on the steering wheel. "Maddie, if you will brush that chip off your shoulder, you'll remember that I not only love your writing, but I have been known to brag about the fact that your newest novel is dedicated to me."

"To your colleagues? You brag to *them*?" She challenged him with a stare.

His averted eyes told her everything she needed to know.

"That's what I thought."

"I bragged on you to my men's group at church and to Ginny and even to the guy at the car wash the other day."

"Well, whoop-dee-doo. But your colleagues in the English department at the university? Did you brag to them? To Milton?"

"I don't remember. Probably."

"Then what does that say about the kind of friends you have? That they would stand in front of you and bash your wife's life-long passion and career? I can't even imag—"

"Don't blame Milton, Maddie."

"Well, don't you defend him!"

"No. What I mean is, Milt *doesn't* know. That you're a writer."

She shook her head, the implication of his words soaking in. "You've never told him? I thought you bragged on me."

The shake of her husband's head was barely perceptible. "I did. Only...it wasn't about your writing."

She took a shuddered breath, and her words came out wobbly. "Are you so ashamed of me that you have to keep what I do a secret? Even from your best friend?"

"I wouldn't say Milton is my best friend." He reached across the console and took her hand. "*You're* my best friend, Maddie."

"Yeah, nice try."

"Well, excuse me for being mistaken about that." He let go of her, his eyes holding a wounded look that tempted her to cave.

But she was not going to let him hijack this offense. *She* was the one who'd been wronged. Who'd been made a fool of. By her own husband. He wasn't getting off that easily. "You know what I mean, Art. And quit trying to change the subject."

"Maddie, I honestly don't know if people at work know you're a writer or not. I wouldn't recommend your books to them anyway. Your books aren't boorish or sloggish enough for that crowd."

"Nice try, buddy. And is sloggish even a word?"

"It is now." His impish smile told her he thought she was starting to thaw.

But he was wrong. "I don't even know how to process this, Art. It couldn't be more clear that you're ashamed of me—not *me*," she quickly corrected before he could beat her to the punch. "But of what I do. Of the kind of books I write."

His jaw tensed and his voice lowered an octave. "Maddie, stop it. You're being ridiculous. None of what you're saying is true and even if it was, you've blown everything completely out of proportion."

"Have I? Put yourself in my place. If you found out that I had been careful not to mention to any of my friends that you're an English prof, you wouldn't be the slightest bit offended?"

He gave a little snort. "What do I care what your friends think?"

"I don't mean *them*. Wouldn't it bother you that *I* wasn't proud of you?"

"I don't think you would have married me if you weren't proud of me. Nor would I have married you if I wasn't incredibly proud of you. I am. And you should know that because I've told you on more than one—"

"If you're so proud of me, then why don't your *esteemed* colleagues know what I do? Why didn't you tell them that tonight when the subject came up?" The anger that rose up in her was completely foreign. And potent. And as Art had said, out of proportion to the offense. Yet she felt powerless to simply shrug it off.

Art tapped the brakes and made a neat three-point turn on the highway. When they were headed back toward home, he spoke in a carefully measured tone. "Maddie, I'm out of my element here. I—" He hesitated. "I'm used to being able to tease a woman out of an argument as ridiculous as this one. Especially one as ridiculous as this. I think maybe we both just need to sleep on it and—"

"What are you saying, exactly? Because it sounds like you're saying that *Annie* would never have acted so immaturely."

"That's *not* what I said. But since you brought it up, no, she would never have let something this petty turn into an hour-long argument."

"Well, excuse me for having feelings. For caring what you think about my life's work. For wanting you to admire me and be proud of me."

"Of course I admire you. And I *am* proud of you. I love you, Annie! Why can't you believe—" He exhaled and his eyes closed briefly as he realized what he'd just said.

The air in the car evaporated.

Maddie tried to breathe, but couldn't, his words cutting like a knife. So the truth came out: It was Annie he admired, Annie he was proud of. Annie he *still* loved.

She waited for him to say something. But he only tightened his grip on the steering wheel.

Her chest ached and she struggled for air. "I am not Annie," she finally managed, each word floating on its own shallow breath. "And I never will be. I'm *sorry* if that disappoints you."

*Three*

S till simmering but also wanting to kick himself, Art pulled into the driveway, chagrined to see all the lights on in the house and their guests moving about behind the sheer curtains in the dining room. At times like this, there were definite disadvantages to owning a bed and breakfast.

He parked in their usual spot at the back of the house and killed the ignition, wishing they had time to hash things through. "Listen, Maddie, I'm truly sorry if—"

She got out of the car and was halfway to the house before he'd barely opened his door. Fine. If that's how she wanted to play it, he'd be the adult in the situation. Still, he'd never seen her like this.

He followed her inside and watched her hurry down the stairs to the little apartment they kept in the inn's basement, completely ignoring the four guests seated around the dining room table.

He pasted on his host-with-the-most smile and cleared his throat. "Welcome, everyone."

The two sixty-something couples turned as one and greeted him. The table was littered with game pieces and soft drink cans, and they were snacking on the mixed nuts and candies Maddie had left out for them.

He gave a little wave. "I'm Art, by the way. Looks like you found the drinks and snacks."

"Oh, we've just made ourselves at home," one of the women said apologetically.

He waved her off. "No, no, that's exactly what we want. Glad you're here."

"Your home is charming." The woman swept a hand toward the front parlor.

"Thank you. Glad you're enjoying it. Will breakfast at eight work for all of you?"

"Thank you," the woman replied, "but we've got a lot of miles to cover tomorrow. We'll just grab something once we get on the road."

"Okay, if you're sure."

The others nodded in agreement.

"Well then, I think I'll hit the hay." Even though he was not a fan of board games, for a minute he was tempted to ask if he could join them. Anything to avoid what awaited him downstairs.

He went into the little kitchen and checked that the coffeemaker was set to brew at seven thirty. As he reached to turn out the lights, his gaze landed on a little teapot that sat beside the sink. Annie's Franciscan Apple teapot that had belonged to her grandmother. Whenever Annie had felt like they needed some time together, she would fill the pot with hot chocolate or chai tea or something she knew he would linger over. And they would sit in this kitchen or out on the porch and sip slowly until they connected again.

He raked his fingers through his hair, still wishing for that swift kick. Not only for accidentally calling his new bride "Annie" but also for his insensitive comment. But what he'd said was true: Annie would *never* have let such mindless comments like the ones Maddie overheard get under her skin. She would have considered the source, shaken off the comments, and moved on. She might even have made excuses for the guilty parties, wondering what had happened in their childhoods to make them so thoughtless or mean. Annabeth Tyler had been the most selfless person he'd ever known.

But it wasn't fair of him to have compared Maddie to her like that. And then to call her by Annie's name. His stomach dropped remembering. Maddie had her own wonderful qualities. They were just a little hard to see right now with the way she was acting. Of course, in her defense, Maddie was younger than Annabeth. And Annie's long illness had granted her maturity and wisdom beyond her years. Still, this wasn't the carefree Maddie he'd fallen in love with.

He eyed the little teapot, not remembering if he'd ever told Maddie its history, but for some reason—maybe she just liked its bright apple pattern as much as Annie had—that teapot had stayed in the same spot near the sink even though Maddie had rearranged much of the rest of the kitchen. He hadn't minded when Maddie put some of Annie's things in storage in exchange for her own dishes and trinkets. But he'd been pleased the teapot remained on the counter, even though they never used it.

He flicked the switch and the kitchen went dark. He checked that the back door was locked, then started downstairs. "Stay up as late as you like," he told his guests. "Just turn out the lights when you retire. You have our number, so text if you need anything." He pointed. "We're just downstairs, so don't hesitate to holler."

He went quietly down the steps, his guests' thank-yous echoing behind him. Steeling himself, he locked the door to their apartment and went looking for Maddie. The small living room was as tidy as they'd left it, a dim floor lamp casting a warm glow in the corner between their reading chairs. Madeleine had gradually transformed this place when she moved in, layering his boring furniture with pillows and throws and creating homey little still lifes on every surface.

They'd talked often about the day they would close the inn, move out of the basement, and start filling the bedrooms with babies. He would turn forty this year and at thirty-four, Maddie said she could literally feel her biological clock ticking. Still, the new contract she'd signed put them much closer to the day they could afford to close the inn. But now he wondered if bringing children into this marriage was even a good idea—assuming she'd ever let him close enough to her again to *make* those aforementioned babies.

He rubbed his face hard with the palms of his hands. Now he was acting as childish as she was. *Attitude check, Tyler*, he admonished himself before padding down the short hallway to their bedroom.

Not surprisingly, Maddie was already asleep—or at least pretending to be—the bedroom lights off except for the one in their ensuite bathroom. He heard Alex's loud purring before he saw the cat—curled in the circle of Maddie's arms. *Traitor*.

Art brushed his teeth and changed out of his clothes then tiptoed to his side of the bed. He glanced at the book on his nightstand. It was a good one and he wanted to read for a few minutes, but if she was awake and just playing possum, that might seem insensitive. So he turned out the bedside lamp and crawled beneath the covers.

While he plumped his pillow and arranged the covers, his wife didn't so much as stir, making him think she was definitely playing possum.

As if in cahoots with Maddie, his stupid cat purred even louder.

Maddie opened her eyes and squinted at the little clock on her nightstand. Eight o'clock? She'd slept in by nearly two hours! Art's side of the bed was cool to the touch. She hadn't heard him get up, but he didn't have an early class on Fridays, so she hoped he'd made breakfast for their guests. She'd heard him talking to them last night after she came down to their apartment. Surely he would have awakened her if she needed to make breakfast. Still, she felt guilty.

She quickly made the bed, showered, and dressed before going upstairs. She was grateful to find the house quiet and the car that had been in the driveway last night gone. Good. Even though she enjoyed the few guests they'd had since their wedding, she would be glad when they were able to close the inn and move out of their little basement apartment. She'd made the apartment as cozy as she knew how, but it was dark down there and she longed for a sunshiny office to write in. Of course, she could always write at the dining room table the way she had in the early days when she'd first started coming to the inn to work.

The memories of those precious days seemed so long ago, and her spirits sank as the memory of their argument last night came crashing back. She tried to push it away, but she could only reach one conclusion: Art had made a mistake marrying her. It was Annie he loved and would always love. She was only a substitute, and a poor one at that.

Even the sign that greeted her every time she turned off of Hampton Road into the driveway reminded her that this house she shared with her husband was still "Annabeth's Inn." And she couldn't count how many times guests had asked if *she* was Annabeth. And then she felt obligated to explain the whole story and accept all the sympathy for Art that came with the territory. How could she possibly compete with the shadow of a veritable saint?

She couldn't. Nor would she. They were married. That knot had been tied and she believed marriage was "'til death do them part," as she'd said in her vows. But she wasn't going to spend the rest of her life trying to coerce Art to forget Annie and fall in love with her. She had more dignity than that.

She felt sick to her stomach. She would be kind to her husband. She would honor the vows they'd made. But she would not pretend things were other than they really were. Nor would she be ashamed of the work she believed God had gifted her to do.

Her cell phone buzzed and she checked her messages. The

most recent was the nursing home asking her to pick up some supplies for her mom. But scrolling down, she saw that at seven a.m., Janice Hudson had left a rather terse text:

*—Give me a call at your earliest possible convenience.*

Her editor was usually forthcoming, and she'd never hesitated to give Maddie news in a text—even bad news. This brief message gave her pause, but it was probably nothing. Maybe she'd forgotten to initial something on the contract.

It was almost ten o'clock in New York, but Janice's text had been sent at eight a.m. Maddie didn't remember hearing her phone around then, but maybe that's what had awakened her. She dialed Janice and pulled out a chair at the dining room table —in case it was bad news.

Her editor answered on the first ring. "Madeleine! Oh, good! I was hoping you got my message."

"Hi, Janice. Is everything okay?"

"Well, that depends on you." An unmistakable smile lit the woman's voice.

"Okay. Depends on me how?" Please, *please* don't tell me you need to move my deadline up.

"Depends on whether you're up for a trip to Paris or not." Maddie could almost see the woman's toothy grin.

"Paris? Don't I wish. But it's just really not in the budget right now. And with my mom's situation and—"

"Wait, let me stop you right there. First of all, this is on our dime. Call it a research trip, since I know that's what you were hoping to be able to do before you started this new series. I won't lie, the schedule Jackson is working on won't leave much time for research, but he's approved the funds if we call it a book tour."

"A book tour? But I don't have any French translations yet. Do I?" To date, all her novels were set in America.

"No, but with so much of this contracted series being set in Paris, we think it'll garner great interest among local bookstores here, so we're already in talks to get your previous novels translated. Jackson feels you could help things along by making a few appearances, get some buzz going before the new series releases."

Maggie didn't even try to hide her excitement. "Bookstore appearances? So you're saying I'd be signing my English language novels? In Paris? Would you be coming with me? If I go, I mean." She'd traveled to Paris eight years ago when she first started writing and had fallen in love with the city. It was where she'd first gotten the idea for this new series, but the publication board had rejected that one until now.

"Slow down, lady." Janice laughed. "One question at a time. Yes, a few book signings. And don't worry, we'll get your books shipped to the stores there. But we're also trying to set up some book club appearances."

"I hope I'd have a translator."

"You wouldn't need one. I've reached out to some American editors I know who are working in France. The book clubs over there love American novels—in English. They read to improve their own English, you know. Like many Parisians, most of the members would already be quite fluent in English."

"Wow... I don't know what to say."

"Say yes, of course. And maybe that handsome husband of yours could come with you. Doesn't he get a spring break? It could be a magnificent second honeymoon."

"But...you'd be coming with me, right?"

A long pause. "Oh, how I wish I could, Madeleine. The thing is, they're maxing out the budget to send you. But don't worry, you'll have a host at each bookshop once you get there. Still, since your hotel would already be paid for, it wouldn't be that much more for Arthur to come with you. On your dime, of course, but it would basically be the price of his airline ticket and meals. And I'll be sure they book a room big enough for both of you. You know how those European hotels can be."

Maddie briefly closed her eyes, running through the possibilities. She wanted to go, of course. But without Art. This might be just the break she needed. *They* needed. But should a couple need a break from each other after barely two months of marriage? She cringed even thinking it. Still, she'd have time alone to figure out how to work through their disagreement. And maybe if she left for a while, he'd miss her and realize—

Realize what? That he'd made a colossal mistake in marrying her? That no one could ever take Annie's place?

She shivered. If that was his conclusion, there wasn't anything she could do about it. And it was clear they both needed time to figure things out. Besides, except for his short spring break that started this weekend, Art would have classes until early May.

"Madeleine, are you there?"

Janice's voice shook her from her musings. "Yes, yes, I'm here. And of course I want to go. I'm honored to have the opportunity."

"Wonderful! How soon could you book your flights?"

"Let me talk to Art tonight. Could I get back to you first thing Monday?"

"Call me at home tomorrow. You have my cell number."

"Okay. Are there any certain dates you have in mind?"

"We can work around your schedule somewhat, but let's make it for three weeks. And it would be really fabulous if you could be there while the city is in bloom. Just think of the lovely photos on your social media."

Such as her online presence was. She needed to step up her game in that regard, but who had time for that when Janice had talked her into an October first deadline with this new contract?

She sighed. "I'll get back to you tomorrow, Janice."

"Marvelous!"

Maddie ended the call and sat staring at her phone, elated at the idea of a chance to do research in Paris, yet at the same time, dreading the conversation she needed to have with Art tonight.

Four

"I doubt there's any way we can get flights in time for spring break." Art frowned, still reeling a little from the news his wife had just delivered. "I wish Janice had let you know about this sooner."

Maddie stirred the batter for a coffee cake she was making for tomorrow's breakfast. "I got the impression they'd only decided to send me recently."

"Well, I guess we can wait until school's out."

She stopped stirring. "I really can't, Art. I don't dare write anything until I've done the research because it's sure to change things, and if I don't start writing until June, there's no way I could make my deadline."

"But I can't take that much time off right after spring break. Maybe Easter. When is Easter this year?" He went to flip through the pages of the new calendar Maddie had hung near the fridge. "No, that won't work either." He refrained from pointing out that she'd signed the contract without any plans to travel to Paris for research.

"Honey, Janice wants me to book as soon as possible. I checked this morning and there's a flight to de Gaulle out of Kansas City a week from today that's only twelve hundred dollars." She tapped the spoon against the side of the bowl, not looking at him. "I mean, they're paying for everything, but I'm sure they don't want to shell out two thousand dollars for the flight."

"So… Maybe I'm wrong, but I'm getting the distinct impression you don't want me to go with you." He'd suspected she was still mad about the faculty gathering fiasco, but was she so upset that she didn't want him along on a three-week overseas trip? Yet, who could blame her? He'd "splurged" on a fancy hotel for their honeymoon to St. Louis. And now her publisher was wooing her with a trip to Paris. Way to make a man feel like a real loser.

"It's not that," she said, pouring the batter into a cake pan. "It's just"—she shrugged— "the timing couldn't be worse."

"Who else is going besides Janice?"

"No one. Just me."

"Wait. But Janice is going with you, right? I mean, you'll at least meet her there?"

She finally turned to face him and waved a sticky spatula in his direction. "I get the impression they're doing this on a low, low budget. I'm just happy they're doing it at all. I thought I was going to have to rely on my last trip for the research."

"It's not like history has changed since you were there last, Maddie."

She gave a humorless laugh. "No, but my memory has."

"Maddie, I do not like the idea of you traipsing around Paris all by yourself."

"I promise not to traipse." She did a fluttery little spin that looked more like a ballerina's pirouette than a traipse, then bit her bottom lip, trying unsuccessfully not to laugh.

But he shook his head. "That's not funny. Things aren't like they were when you were there before."

"What do you mean?"

"This world is going to you-know-where in a you-know-what. It's not safe anywhere, love. Especially not for an American woman traveling alone."

"Art, it's not like this is my first trip abroad. I felt perfectly safe when I was there before."

"That was eight years ago, Maddie. Things have changed."

"I know, but I'll be in the city the whole time. Janice knows some American editors there, and she said I'd have an escort once my book events start. I'm sure I'll be well taken care of." She sprinkled a cinnamon mixture over the batter and popped the cake pan into the oven.

He blew out a sigh. "Well, I can see it doesn't matter what I think."

"Of course it does." She ran steaming water into the bowl, glancing back at him. "But I'm not a child, Art. As I'm pretty sure you know, I did some traveling before I met you. I know how to take care of myself. I know what to watch for. You don't need to worry. And I'm not going to be gone that long anyway."

He turned the chair around and straddled it backward, watching her. "So how long is not that long?"

She turned back to face the sink, suddenly preoccupied with the dirty dishes. "Janice said at least two weeks. Maybe three."

"Three weeks? No way. You would leave me for three weeks? That's almost longer than we've been married!" He didn't know whether to be mad or hurt. Maybe he was both.

"That's a bit of an exaggeration, honey."

"Not much." He tried a different tack. "What about your mom? You wouldn't leave her for that long, would you?"

She came to sit in the chair across the table from him. "I thought about that. And I do feel bad leaving her that long, but honestly, Art, she's well taken care of at the home. I don't think she'll even realize I'm gone. If she can remember who I am."

"She knows who you are, Maddie. Even when she can't verbalize it, you can see it in her eyes. She lights up when you walk in."

Maddie gave a little laugh. "I think it's *you* she's lighting up for. But I will try to keep the trip as short as possible."

"For your mom? Or for me? Because I *will* know you're gone."

She threw him a look. "For both of you, of course. And don't worry, I'll make some breakfast casseroles and coffee cakes and put them in the freezer. All you'll have to do is remember to take them out the night before if we have guests."

"That's not why I don't want you to go."

"I know, but I don't want to leave you hanging either. I'm sure Ginny would be willing to help out if you needed something too. She'd probably jump at the chance to play hostess if you have a meeting or just need some help."

He scoffed. "Ginny is nearly eighty-five years old. I'm not going to impose on her. I ran this place by myself for two and a half years. I think I can manage."

She reached to put her hand over his. "I know you can. I just thought—" She didn't finish the sentence and instead gave a little shake of her head and went back to the sink.

He sat there for several minutes watching her. He loved this woman. From the tendrils of hair that escaped from the clasp and brushed her swan-like neck to the curve of her hips to her pink-toed bare feet. He loved her heart. Oh, she could be maddeningly infuriating at times. And they were as different as cornbread and croissants. For that matter, Maddie and Annie were as different as cornbread and croissants.

Still, from the moment he'd discovered that the pretty girl from the post office was the eloquent creature who'd been staying at his inn, there'd never been any doubt. Truth was, he'd fallen in love with her from the notes she'd left at the inn each day and had only fallen deeper in love after they'd begun to spend time face to face.

So why were they sitting in this kitchen discussing a three-week separation when they'd barely been married twice that long? Not that he'd even thought of marrying again until he met Maddie, but this—at least so far—wasn't at all what he'd expected. And it wasn't fair to her, but what he'd expected was a marriage like he'd had with Annie. One where they spent almost every minute they weren't working *together*. One where she was always available to him, not locked away in some room writing for hours on end with a "Do Not Disturb" sign on the door! And now Maddie had signed a contract for three more books.

He didn't want her to think he resented her success. But… maybe he did. Just a little. Not the success itself but the fact that it took her away from him. And now she was headed to Paris for three weeks without him. But maybe that would be better than having her on the other side of a wall in the house they shared, locking him out.

He rose and scooted the chair back under the table. "I'm going downstairs."

Before he reached the doorway, something crashed behind him. He heard Maddie gasp and whirled to find her kneeling, shards of pottery in a pile in front of her. She looked up at him, eyes wide. "Oh, Art. I'm so sorry. I didn't mean— I don't know what—"

In that moment, he realized what had broken. The apple teapot Annie had loved so much. Anger, grief, disappointment, and a flood of other emotions he couldn't even identify rushed to the forefront. "What did you *do*?" The caustic whisper came out more accusing than he'd intended.

"Oh, Art." She covered her mouth with her hands. "I'm so sorry. It was an accident. My sleeve must have caught on it and—"

Even the horrified look on Maddie's face wasn't enough to keep his temper in check.

"I'm sorry," she said again. "I am *so* sorry." She picked up two larger shards, trying to fit one to the other as if she could somehow put Annie's treasured teapot back together.

"Leave it," he said, trying—and failing—to soften his tone. "You'll cut yourself—"

She gasped, and as if fulfilling his prophecy, she held up her hand and stared at the red gash across her index finger.

"Leave it," he said again. "It's beyond fixing."

"I promise I didn't mean to, Art. It was an accident. My sleeve must have caught—"

"It doesn't matter. I'll clean it up."

"Let me help you. I can—"

"Go take care of your hand. Please. Just go."

With tears in her eyes, she left the room.

He knew he should speak words that absolved her. Knew he should comfort her, forgive her. But right now, he couldn't. Right now, he felt as if he'd lost the very last piece of Annie that remained.

And he didn't much like what stood in her place.

Maddie stuffed another jacket in her carry-on, closed the lid and sat on it, trying to zip it up underneath her. Not even close. She opened the bag again, took out a pair of shoes, rearranged everything, and tried again. It zipped, but just barely.

"Need some help there?"

She turned to see Art standing in the doorway watching her. She wished she could read his thoughts, but his enigmatic expression told her nothing. It was almost worse than the potent mixture of disappointment and anger on his face a week ago as he looked down at Annie's precious teapot shattered on the kitchen floor. At least then there had been no doubt what he was thinking and feeling toward her.

He'd apologized more than once, and she'd forgiven him more than once. Every day she'd forgiven him anew. But that didn't mean it didn't still hurt. She pushed away the dark shadows of those memories and forced a smile. "I think I got it. I just hope I'm not forgetting anything."

"If you did, you can just buy a replacement when you get there. I still think you should wait until you get to Paris and buy some new clothes there."

"I don't want to risk it. And Janice has my calendar so full, I don't know when I'm supposed to get any research done, let alone go shopping." The truth was, she had two full days in the city before her first book club appearance, but Art would only worry if he knew she was wandering the city alone, poking around old museums and even older cemeteries.

Art didn't respond but stared out the window to the drab prairie beyond.

"Are you okay?" They'd exchanged pleasant—if mostly meaningless—conversations throughout the week, yet Maddie felt they'd reached an unspoken truce on some level. He wasn't happy about her going, but he admitted it would be foolish for her to pass up this opportunity. She didn't think he guessed her ulterior motive for going without him.

He nodded, then reached out to her. "Hey… Come here." He gathered her into his arms. "I love you. You know that, don't you?"

Tears puddled behind her eyelids. When she could speak, she whispered, "I'll miss you." That was true. And part of her desperately wanted to call Janice this minute and cancel the whole thing. But maybe some time apart would help them both see things more clearly.

She hadn't told him she loved him since their fight the night of the faculty gathering. They'd made love only once since then and though it had held all the physical passion it always had, she'd cried herself to sleep afterward, wondering, agonizing over whether it was even *her* he'd been thinking of.

But she *did* love him. Oh, how she loved him. Still, she wanted to give him space to grieve Annie, grieve the fact that his new wife wasn't and never could be the perfect, beloved wife he'd lost.

She needed to grieve the fact that their love for each other would probably always be lopsided. They would probably always disagree about her career, how much she traveled, how many hours she spent holed up in her office writing, and of course, the fact that, in his eyes, she wrote the despicable genre of popular fiction—she mentally rolled her eyes—and at least according to Art, hers wasn't even popular.

It still stung to think about the conversation she'd overheard that night at the president's home. Not because of the comments Art's colleagues had made—there would always be people who didn't respect her genre—but because he hadn't come to her defense.

But that he'd called her by Annie's name? That had to mean something. Added to all the rest, it was too much to ignore.

Still, she'd forgiven him for that too. And had told him as much. But she wasn't sure she could ever fully trust him with her gift again. Though he claimed to have fallen in love with her through her words, she knew now that it was only because *Annie* had found her words touching, healing. Art had read her manuscript grudgingly and only to help out an "old" friend of Ginny's. And he'd only enjoyed what she wrote because his beloved Annie had enjoyed it.

That was forgivable. Understandable. But that didn't mean it didn't hurt like crazy to realize the truth. And *that* would take some time to process.

*Five*

"Please let me know when you land safely." Standing near the curb at the airport, Art pulled her into a tight hug. The driver of the car behind them laid on the horn.

"I will." Maddie wanted to cry.

"I need to go, love."

"I know."

He tipped her chin up, forcing her to look at him. "I love you." He kissed her again, then pulled away.

She turned and feigned concern about the zippers on her carry-on bag so he wouldn't see the tears that blinded her. She'd resolved not to give him one more reason to accuse her of "blowing everything out of proportion." But the truth was, she wanted to leave her luggage on the curb, hop back in the pickup, and return to Clayburn with him. She'd made a terrible mistake agreeing to go on this trip without him. How could they ever work things out if they weren't even together?

They were newlyweds, and regardless of whether Art had regrets, they'd agreed from the beginning that divorce would never be an option for them. It wasn't as if he could ever have Annie back, and Maddie was determined to do whatever it took to make a happy marriage. So why was she about to get on a flight that would take her halfway across the world alone for three weeks?

The horn blared again. She hooked her purse over the handle of her carry-on. "Go. I'll let you know when I'm there."

"Don't forget."

"I won't." She forced herself to smile and meet his eyes. "You let me know too, okay?"

"I will." He'd likely be home before her plane took off. And he'd be in bed again before she landed in Paris.

She wheeled her carry-on around and started for the closest terminal door. But something made her turn back. Art gave the impatient driver an apologetic wave and started to climb behind the wheel.

"Art! Arthur!" Her breath caught and she could barely get his name out.

His head came up and he looked at her over the hood of his pickup, a question in his eyes.

"I love you!" It came out on a sob.

The slow smile that came in response seemed filled with regret and—dare she hope, *relief*? Maybe even affection. It melted her and gave her the courage to turn and continue toward the wide airport door.

"Hurry home, love," he called behind her.

The trip home from the airport was one of the loneliest Art could remember since he'd driven home from taking Annie's brother to the airport after her funeral. The Kansas prairie wore its ugliest brown jacket and spring seemed a long way away. But mostly he longed for Maddie. And for Annie, if he was honest. Was it possible to love two women at the same time?

He thought he'd worked through all this before he and Maddie said their vows. Why was it rearing its ugly head again now? His rational self knew that his earthly relationship with

Annie—their marriage—had appropriately ended when she went to heaven nearly three years ago. And he had no doubt that God had put Maddie in his life as a precious gift. And he did love Maddie with all his heart. He just needed to sort out the feelings of guilt and confusion he had whenever memories of Annie encroached on their new marriage.

Maddie was always so good to honor Annie's memory. And it really did help that Annie's love of Madeleine Houser's novels had been a big part of what brought Maddie to him. How well he remembered the night he'd discovered Annie's markings on the pages of Maddie's novels. It had felt like her approval. But had he moved forward too quickly despite everything?

He quashed the thought. Whether he'd rushed into things or not, he was married to Maddie now, and they had agreed from the beginning that divorce would not be a part of their vocabulary. No matter what. He'd meant that. And now it was time to move forward and work on making this new marriage all God intended it to be. But that was hard to do when his bride was winging her way across an ocean nearly five thousand miles from him.

As if in reply, a text dinged and Maddie's face appeared on his screen. He had the interstate almost to himself and risked a quick look at her message.

—*Boarding now. I love you.*

The words made him remember how she'd turned and shouted those same words at the airport. It was the first time she'd said them in a long while. She was no doubt worrying that something might happen to one of them before she returned in three weeks. Still, her words warmed him.

*Nearly three weeks.* Such an eternity given how tenuous things had been between them recently. He was only an hour from home, but he exited at Emporia and pulled into a gas station parking lot to reply to her message. He didn't want her to worry that something had happened to him—or that he was holding a grudge. He hated texting. Had always preferred a pen and paper —especially since that was how he and Maddie had met and fallen in love—but absent that option now, he tapped out a brief message, then hit Send.

*—I love you, too, Maddie. Have a wonderful time! Let me know the minute you get there.*

Eager to be home, he didn't wait for a reply but made a mental note to check his messages once he was there. He would be sawing logs by the time she landed in Paris. But if she hadn't yet gotten his message before she took off, at least it would be waiting for her when she landed.

He imagined her relieved sigh and a small smile growing on her pretty face as she read his words.

Yes, he loved Madeleine Houser. It might take time to grow into the deep love he and Annie had known. But they *had* time. They had the rest of their lives.

The lights on the runway at Charles de Gaulle reflected back on themselves in the rain. Maddie stared out onto the wet asphalt as the plane taxied to a halt. After the seatbelt sign went off, she gathered her belongings, and while she waited for her seatmates to gather their things and let her into the aisle, she checked her phone messages.

She smiled reading Art's message she'd gotten before takeoff. There was another *I love you* sent probably before he'd gone to bed. Her phone had already switched over to Paris time.

She knew he'd have his phone turned on atop his bedside table. But she didn't want to wake him, so she made a mental note to text him later. She'd managed to sleep for a few hours of the ten-hour flight, but she was eager to get to her hotel for a good night's sleep before she set out on her research first thing tomorrow.

As she stepped onto the train platform half an hour later, fond memories of her last trip to Paris flooded her. She'd been with friends from college on a bus tour that time, but it had been special because it had been the beginning of her writing career. Even though she hadn't sold the Paris stories until recently, Paris was where she'd first gotten confirmation that her writing was good enough to be published. First from her friends, and soon after from Janice, who'd written her a lovely, encouraging rejection letter sent via the postal service with a pretty Statue of Liberty postage stamp—her first clue that she was going to love Janice Hudson.

Even as she waited outside the airport for the cab Art had insisted she book ahead of time, Maddie snapped pictures and took notes. Most of her story was set in the Paris of 1897, but Janice had asked her to write dual timeline novels with this new series, so there would be scenes from present-day Paris in her novel too. After Janice had rejected her original proposal for a novel about the tragic Paris fire just before the turn of the century at the Bazar de la Charité, she'd agreed to write about the Great Chicago Fire. But since signing the contract, she'd second-guessed herself. Could she make these new novels different enough from her last series when both of them dealt with tragic fires? Would she be locking herself into a reputation as an author who only wrote about fiery conflagrations?

Well, it was too late now. The contract was signed, the advance monies paid, and here she was in Paris. *Fantastique!*

It was approaching sunset when the taxi dropped her off in front of what looked like a seedy, narrow alley in Paris's 1st arrondissement.

"Grand Hôtel Dechampaigne? Est-ce l'hôtel?" Her French, such as it was, was even rustier than she'd realized.

But the driver was patient and spoke passable English. "Oui, madame. Rue Jean Lantier." He pointed to the street sign on the side of a building that read the same. "C'est une courte distance."

"There?" She followed his gaze. "Down this alley?"

"Oui. La ruelle. A short walk to the hotel." He switched to English and nodded with a wink. "Our streets are not wide like your city, non? "

"Non," she admitted sheepishly. "Merci."

She peeled a ten euro note from the stack in her wallet as a tip, hoping it was generous.

His smile said it was. He thanked her and sped away.

The buildings on either side cast dark shadows across the street, but she could make out two young men leaning against the taller building on the left. The tips of the cigarettes they smoked glowed red and receded in unison.

With trepidation, she started down the alley, keeping her phone in one hand in case she needed to call for help. Although she couldn't remember France's equivalent of 9-1-1. It was some combination of 1s and 2s, she thought. Some help that would be in an emergency.

She wheeled her carry-on around to her left side forming a barricade between her and the men and hurried past, trying to look like she knew where she was going. They ignored her, but she felt their eyes on her back after she'd passed.

At the corner of the building, the street jagged slightly, and just then, to her great relief, a five-story hotel loomed in front of her. The entrance of the triangular building jutted into the street, its red awning brightly lit underneath. As she approached, automatic doors slid open and welcomed her in.

She hurried through a second set of doors, waiting for her eyes to adjust. The cozy wood-paneled room boasted a vintage tile floor, but various layered carpets protected it from the foot traffic it likely received.

She crossed to the reservation desk where a man wearing a maroon Indian kurta sat scrolling on his cell phone. "Bonjour. A reservation for Madeleine Houser, s'il vous plaît?"

He looked up. "Of course, Madame."

She piled her things on the high desktop in front of her and fished out her credit card. He scanned the card and said something in French that she didn't understand.

But before she could ask him to repeat it, he handed her card back, opened a drawer, and selected a key. He gave her the large oval keychain that bore the hotel's name and her room number, 104. She made a note to guard the key with her life, since she didn't relish the idea of someone finding it on the street somewhere and knowing exactly which door that key opened.

The clerk pointed past the small bar next to the reservation desk. He said something about the elevator, but her expression must have revealed that she was not following his French, and she was relieved when he continued his spiel in English. "The lift is to your right and the stairs, if you prefer, are just around the corner before you reach the breakfast room."

She remembered then that European first floors were actually on the second floor, not ground level.

"Our breakfast buffet is served every morning beginning at seven, and eight on Sunday." As he told her about the hotel's other services, the elevator door opened, and a rather large man extricated himself and an equally large suitcase from the tiny space. Turning back to the clerk, she was thankful she'd decided not to check a bag. "I believe I'll take the stairs."

"When you go out, Madame, simply leave your key with me at the desk. You may pick it up right here on your return. For your safety," he explained.

"Oh. Yes, thank you. I will. Merci."

A man in line behind her cleared his throat pointedly.

She quickly gathered her things and rounded the corner to the lounge area, then lugged her bags up the uneven carpeted stairs. The wide staircase curved, then narrowed before opening directly onto a hallway. She found the door with her room number on it and quietly turned the key.

While the outside of the hotel belied the claim of being historic, her little suite looked delightfully ancient. The far wall was old stone, with a casement window that looked out over the street. She pushed back the red velvet curtains and cranked open the French casement window. A puff of cool spring air gently stirred the white lace valance, carrying in the spicy scent of some street vendor's culinary offerings. Her view was the tall building next door across from where the two young men had been smoking, but she didn't care. She was in the heart of the city, and she had nearly three weeks to explore Paris to her heart's content.

The small bathroom was tiled floor to ceiling in square maroon tiles that looked as if they might have been added in the 1940s. Perhaps that was when the hotel had been built, though that would hardly qualify as historic for this city.

She started to put her things away in the drawers of the antique bureau but fatigue overcame her. Instead, she quickly brushed her teeth, then crawled beneath the crisp sheets. *Oh, heavenly.* The alarm clock on the nightstand read eight o'clock. That was one o'clock in the afternoon in Kansas. Art would be teaching a class right now. She should text him so he'd have a message waiting when his class was over. She raised up on one elbow, looking for her purse. It was right where she'd dropped it on a bow-legged secretary desk against the stone wall. She started to get up, then plopped back onto the pillow, too weary to crawl out of this comfy bed.

The cacophony of the city outside her open window became a lulling white noise, and her eyelids grew heavy. *She was in Paris.* It all seemed as surreal as it had the first time. She'd rest for a few minutes, then text Art before she went out to find something for supper.

Six

Exiting Perry Hall, Art hiked his backpack up on one shoulder and checked the messages on his phone. Nothing from Maddie. Surely her flight had landed by now. He lengthened his stride and headed across campus to the faculty parking lot, dialing her as he went.

It went straight to voicemail, and he tried not to sound frustrated when he recorded his third message. "Hey, love? Where are you? Praying you had a good flight. Call me as soon as you get this."

The campus bustled with students heady with the spring sunshine, summer vacation so close they could almost touch it. Art dodged Frisbees and an errant baseball as he crossed the commons, walking briskly as if he could stave off the familiar melancholy threatening to envelop him. He'd once shared his students' optimism with the coming of spring.

That was before a horrific April three years ago. Annabeth had thought it a gift that God saw fit to end her cancer journey during her favorite month of the year. And maybe she was right. It would have been awful to head into winter with a grief so fresh. Annie's birthday had been in April too, so in the month ahead, while the world burst into bloom, he faced two hard days.

At his car, he checked his phone again. Still nothing. Maddie should definitely have landed by now. But maybe her flight was delayed out of Kansas City after she'd told him they were boarding. It wouldn't be the first time that had happened.

He drove through for hamburgers to eat on the way home. He had to get beds ready for three guest rooms—a full house for three nights. At least that would make the days go quickly.

Maddie had cleaned the bathrooms and dusted the bedrooms before she left—a sacrifice he deeply appreciated—especially since she'd been busy getting ready for this trip. But it fell to him to make the beds and figure out something to go with the breakfast casseroles Maddie had left in the freezer. He'd taken Maddie's help for granted these last weeks since their marriage. She always did the tasks around the inn so cheerfully. He made a mental note to tell her how much he appreciated that when she called.

At her suggestion, they'd been booking more rooms during the week to bring in a little extra money. With her new contract, they were more than comfortable, but they wanted to pad their savings account toward the day they could close the inn and make the entire house their home. "Fill it with babies," she always said.

He wondered now if that was a good idea but quickly banished the thought, determined to be more positive. Which Maddie had made easier with her parting words. Still, why hadn't she called?

He finished his burgers and fries as he pulled into the driveway. After tossing the empty wrappers into the trash can, he checked his phone again. Still nothing.

He checked the airline's website and confirmed that her flight had landed. On time. He dialed her again. Straight to voicemail. He didn't know what to add beyond what he'd said in his other messages, so he just hung up. A frisson of alarm tinged his spine. She should have arrived at her hotel hours ago. And if plans changed, she should have let him know what was going on. She knew he would worry until he heard from her. He'd worry after he heard from her too, but she didn't need to know that.

Maybe she'd posted something on one of her social media accounts. He rarely even logged on to his own, but he did so now and checked Maddie's accounts for posts. Nothing there either. The last thing she'd posted was a teaser showing her luggage by the inn's front door with Alex, tail high, sniffing the backpack lopped over her suitcase handle. Posted two days ago, the photo caption said, "Something exciting is in the works. Allez! On y va!" He couldn't translate the French words, but she must have photographed her empty luggage because she hadn't finished packing until the last minute.

Inside, he went from room to room, changing sheets and plumping pillows the way Annie had taught him, then standing in the doorway and looking at each room with a critical eye the way Maddie had taught him. The room looked welcoming enough. A memory came of one night when he and Maddie had been making up the beds in this room together and a pillow fight had ensued. One that ended downstairs in *their* bedroom. He could almost hear Maddie's playful laughter and it brought a smile and a twinge of longing.

Why hadn't she called?

Glancing at the clock in the upstairs hallway, he realized it was almost midnight in Paris. Alarmed, he dialed again and let out a breath of relief when it didn't go directly to voicemail. But the voice that answered sent a boulder into the pit of his stomach.

"Bonsoir. Recherchez-vous la personne à qui appartient ce téléphone?"

"What? I'm sorry. Could you speak English please?"

"Oui, of course. Are you seeking the owner of this telephone?"

"Yes. Yes, I'm calling for Madeleine Tyler."

"Non, I am sorry. There is no one here by that name."

"Here? Where are you?"

"I am with the hotel, Monsieur."

*What was going on?* He hadn't dialed the hotel. "I am calling for Madeleine Tyler." Then it struck him. "Perhaps she's registered as Madeleine Houser?"

"Ah, oui. Madame Houser is at this location. This must be her cell phone?"

"Yes. Let me speak to her, please." Janice had probably booked Maddie under the Houser name. He wouldn't read anything into that. But why was a strange Frenchman answering Maddie's phone?

"I'm sorry, I must ask who is calling?"

"Who is *this*? And why is she not answering her own phone?" He hadn't meant for it to come out so rudely, but something wasn't right.

"I am Monsieur Bajwa. The lady left her phone at the front desk."

"The front desk?"

"Oui, at her hotel of course, Monsieur. The Grand Hôtel Dechampaigne."

"Could you put her on, please? I would like to speak with her." Why on earth would Maddie have left her phone at the hotel's front desk?

"I believe Madame has retired for the night."

Art had to bite his tongue to keep from shouting. With great restraint, he spoke slowly and clearly. "Please get my wife. It is urgent that I speak with her."

"Un moment, s'il vous plaît. I will get her."

"Thank you. Merci," he repeated, wanting to stay in the man's good graces until he was sure Maddie was all right. He ran downstairs and grabbed a notepad and pen from a kitchen drawer, then went to the dining room table. He pulled out a chair and sat, waiting.

It seemed an eternity before the phone came to life again, but when it did, it was Maddie's sleepy voice he heard. But she wasn't talking to him.

"Yes? Bonjour. Is something wrong?"

"Is this your phone, Madame? You left it at the front desk. It must have been hidden by les journaux—er, the newspapers."

"Oh, good heavens. Thank you. I hadn't even missed it. What time is it anyway?"

"It is precisely eleven forty-nine, Madame."

"Maddie? Maddie!" Art tried to get her attention, but she and Monsieur whatever-his-name-was were having a grand old time getting to know each other.

"Oh, excusez-moi. Your husband is on the line."

"Art? Oh!" A clattering, a rustling, and finally she was there. "Art?"

"Maddie. Is everything okay? Why didn't you call?"

"Art?" she repeated. "What time is it?"

"Well, it's almost five here in Kansas, but I guess it's midnight there. You should have gotten to Paris hours ago! I've been calling since I got out of class. Four hours ago!"

"Oh, honey! I'm so sorry." Another commotion. "Thank you, Monsieur Bajwa."

"Maddie?"

"Oui, merci. Um...Art?"

"I'm here."

"Oh, honey, I'm sorry. I got to the hotel, and I was going to call you, and then—I just crashed. But I'm here safe and sound. Everything is fine."

Both relieved and annoyed, he tried not to show it. "You go back to sleep then. I'm sorry I woke you."

"I don't know if I can sleep now."

"You don't want to stay up all night. You'll be double jet-lagged if you do that."

"How is everything in Kansas? Have the guests arrived?"

"Not yet, but I got the beds made up. Everything's ready for them." An awkward silence grew between them. "So, what's on your agenda for tomorrow?"

"I'm going to a chapel, Notre-Dame-de-Consolation. It's on the site of the fire I'm writing about."

"Ah. So you're taking a cab?"

"Actually, I'll probably walk. It's not far and that way I can see where my characters would have walked. The Musée d'Orsay is on the way, so I'll probably stop there too."

"Please be careful. I hate that you're there alone. I miss you."

"I'll be fine, Art. I'm excited to see the city. See how it's changed since I was here last."

No *I miss you, too* or *I wish you were here.* Just chattering on about how excited she was to be far away from him. A sick feeling settled in his gut. "Well, just be sure you get back to the hotel before dark, okay?"

"I'll be fine, Art. I've been here before."

"And hang on to your phone. What happened with that anyway?"

She giggled nervously. "I'm not sure. I must have left it on the counter when I checked in at the hotel. I'm sorry I didn't call you. I just crashed."

"Yes, that's what you said. You're lucky your phone wasn't stolen."

"I promise I'll be more careful."

"I hope so. What would you even *do* if you lost your phone?"

"I'm not going to lose my phone, Art. But if I did, I'd use my laptop to find it or I'd find a shop, buy a new phone, and be back in business." Her tone bordered on smug.

"You make it sound so easy. By the time you could do all that, our bank accounts would be cleaned out and your identity would belong to someone else."

"That's not going to happen, honey. I will be careful. Please don't worry."

She was not taking any of this seriously enough. But there was nothing he could do about it from here. "Just be careful," he repeated. "I'll let you get back to sleep now. Please call me when you wake up though."

"You want me to call you at midnight? Your midnight?"

"Oh. No, I guess not. But call me when you get back from

your research trip tomorrow. Or the next day, or whatever time it is here when you get back."

"That will be..." He could picture her furrowed forehead as she tried to calculate.

He did the math for her. "Around ten a.m. here."

"You'll be in class."

"Oh. Yeah, I guess I will." So when in blazes were they ever supposed to talk? He couldn't suppress the sigh that came. "I guess I'll talk to you in three weeks when you get home."

"Art..." She made his name two syllables and gave a hollow laugh. "It's two and a half weeks. And we'll figure it out, honey. I'll text you."

Outside the kitchen window, dusk had fallen and a car pulled into the driveway, its headlights illuminating the *Annabeth's Inn* sign at the edge of the front lawn. For the first time, Art wondered if it bothered Maddie to see Annie's name in six-inch letters every time they pulled into the driveway.

"Art? Honey, you there?"

"I'm here. Okay...well, I think our guests just arrived. I'd better go. Get some sleep. I'm glad you made it safely."

"Goodnight, honey. I love you." She sounded so matter-of-fact.

He wished he'd FaceTimed her so he could see her expression. "You too, Maddie. Sleep well, love." He clicked off his phone and placed it on the charger by the back door.

Alex appeared in the doorway and cocked his head as if asking a question. "She's fine, buddy. I don't think she even misses us."

Seven

The wail of sirens roused Maddie from a sound sleep. Not the sirens of a sheriff's car speeding by on a Kansas road but the *eee-ooo-eee-ooo* of a Parisian police car on cobbled streets. She rolled out of bed and went to close the window, which she'd left open a few inches so she could fall asleep to the sounds of the city at night. She even loved the sound of that siren, fading into the distance now, so much gentler than American police sirens.

She checked her phone, chagrined to remember how she'd carelessly left it on the hotel counter. It was just past five a.m. Paris time. She'd slept at least eight hours counting her long nap before Art had awakened her.

No messages from him yet this morning. It would be...after ten p.m. in Kansas? She checked the world clock on her phone to confirm. Art went to bed early during the week and probably more so now since he would be getting up even earlier than usual to fix breakfasts. A pang of guilt caught her, and for a minute she wished she could be back at the inn scrambling eggs while he fried bacon, brushing past each other, stealing kisses as they worked around each other in the small kitchen.

But that had been before. Tears came to her eyes. She missed him. Was he missing her too? Or was he just relieved to have back the quiet of his life before she'd complicated everything. She was being dramatic. She knew that. They'd had a lovely honeymoon period of getting to know each other, relishing the gift of a relationship neither of them had been looking for.

He wasn't completely innocent, but she carried the biggest burden of guilt for putting a swift end to their carefree days. She never should have let Art's thoughtlessness become a mountain between them. It wasn't the end of the world that he'd called her by Annie's name. It wasn't even that hard to understand how confusing it must be for him to get accustomed to a new love when his first love had been so very sweet. Why hadn't she told him the things she was thinking now before everything got blown out of proportion?

*Blown out of proportion.* The very words Art had used the night everything had started going south. She looked at her phone, tempted to call him even though it might wake him up. But no, it was late in Kansas, and he would for sure be asleep. He was only being thoughtful not to call or text her since he'd already awakened her from a dead sleep only a few hours ago. Not to mention Art was not a fan of texting.

Still, she longed to hear his voice. To hear in his tone, in the way he said her name, that everything was okay between them. Or at least would be.

With a sigh, she pulled the spread up over the bed and went to get in the shower. The Musée d'Orsay awaited her. And the cathedral where her characters had lived—and died. Oh, this new series would be so much better because she'd have a fresh chance to walk these ancient streets and especially to explore the Paris her contemporary characters would have lived in.

Last night, with new ideas for her novel swirling in her head, she'd been distracted from worrying about how she and Art could ever find their way back to what they'd once had together. But it all came crashing back this morning. Was he still frustrated with her? Was he relieved to have her gone and things back to the way they'd been before he met her? Being so far away made it too easy to imagine the worst. That her husband was full of regrets, wishing he could go back and undo his decision to marry her. And five thousand miles from home, there wasn't a thing she could do about it except pray. But even God seemed distant and remote.

Art's cell phone buzzed again. Finally. He'd started to wonder if Maddie had any intention of responding to his texts. His imagination had gotten the best of him, creating scenarios in which his wife simply disappeared in Paris. He picked up his phone, but before he read the message, he took a deep breath and reminded himself to be kind. He would save the fight for when she got home.

He turned his phone over. Not Maddie. Instead, it was the guest from you-know-where. For the third time—so far.

*—So sorry to bother you again, Arthur, but I'm not finding any bar soap in our bathroom. My husband is allergic to most body washes and we just don't want to risk it. Do you have some bar soap we could borrow?*

He gave a low growl and muttered, "Lady, if I give you a bar of my soap, I do not want it back." How hard would it be to toss a bar of soap in their suitcase since they knew the guy was allergic? But grudgingly, he tapped out the reply he knew Maddie would have written:

*—Of course! No problem. I'll bring a bar right up. I'll just put it outside your door.*

He hit send.

The reply was almost instantaneous. The woman must be voice texting.

*—Oh my! We don't need a bar. My husband already had two beers at the clubhouse. LOL! Sorry, I couldn't resist! Teehee. But thank you so much. I'll watch for the bar (of soap!)*

Oh brother. Okay, that did it. He'd used up all his nice on this woman. And he was done waiting for Maddie to reply to the three texts he'd sent, all of which had gone unanswered. He tapped her number and started upstairs in search of a bar of soap, not even surprised when her phone went to voicemail. Again.

Maddie's eyes flew open when her cell phone vibrated in her purse on the pew beside her. She looked around the sanctuary, hoping no one else could hear it. The very air in the chapel was hushed. Notre-Dame-de-Consolation at 17 Rue Jean-Goujon was in the 8th arrondissement, built on the very ground where the Bazar de la Charité had been—the site of the fire that would be the center-piece of her novel. Letting the silence transport her to 1897 Paris, she could almost hear the excited buzz of the crowd anticipating the start of the annual charity bazaar orchestrated by the French Catholic aristocracy.

In her mind's eye, a new opening scene for her novel played out before her as the research she'd already done pulled her back through the years. The towering stone walls of the chapel slowly fell away, and in their place stood the expansive wooden ware-house that once occupied this piece of now-sacred ground. The warehouse that organizers had artfully transformed into a medieval street using scraps of painted wood, fabric, cardboard, and papier-maché. A nightmare of a tinderbox waiting to be ignited by a newfangled attraction—the recently patented Cine-matographe that used ether lamps to illuminate and project moving images.

She pictured mothers and daughters, grandfathers and grand-daughters, dressed in their finest—and tragically, most flammable —spring finery. Starched blouses and crinoline petticoats beneath the ladies' skirts. Likely not one of them had an inkling as they'd dressed that morning that it would be their last day on earth.

Her phone vibrated again. *Argh!* Terrible timing. But it was probably Art and he'd be worrying about her. Sadly, she knew from experience that if she didn't get these images and impressions down on paper, the small but vital details that gave life to a story would be lost.

She checked her phone, trying her best to stay in her fictional world. But notifications—three texts and a voicemail from Art— yanked her back to the present. Had something happened at home? She flipped to her Kansas clock. It was four a.m. back home!

She gathered her things and rose quietly, hurrying outside. Without taking time to read his texts, she dialed Art and waited, heart pounding.

"Well, there you are! Good morning, love."

She breathed a sigh of relief at his cheery greeting. "What are you doing up? It's almost four in the morning."

"Couldn't sleep. And I knew you'd be out and about. Were you able to get back to sleep...after I called?"

"I slept a little bit." It was only fifteen minutes, but she didn't want to make him feel bad.

"So how's it going today?"

"It's lovely, Art. I walked to the chapel this morning, and the apple and cherry blossoms are about to pop all over the city. It's just gorgeous and it smells heavenly. When they're all in full bloom in a few days, it's going to be unbelievable! I'll send pictures. In fact, I need to post something online for my readers today."

"Well, don't tell anyone where you're staying or anything."

"No, of course not." Did he think she was a complete idiot? But no. She had that coming. After all, she *had* "lost" her phone the very first day. She changed the subject. "After breakfast at the hotel, I walked to the chapel. The weather was perfect and it is so gorgeous here with all the trees budding out. And I'm getting so much good stuff for my book."

"That's wonderful. I'm glad. Are you getting any writing done?"

"Honey, I just got here. When you woke— When you *called* me, I'd just gotten in. I went straight to bed, as you know, and then I left the hotel right after breakfast. It's almost lunch time here."

"I don't like being in different time zones."

"I know. It makes me a little crazy."

His voice dropped. "I'll tell you what makes me a little crazy."

"What?"

"You not being here with me. I miss you."

The longing in his voice warmed her. "I miss you too. But the time will go fast."

"For you maybe. The days are dragging here."

"I've barely been gone twenty-four hours, Art. But maybe the days wouldn't seem so long if you didn't get up at four a.m.," she teased.

He laughed and she felt as if she'd given him a gift.

"So you walked to the cathedral—or wherever you are?"

"It's just a small chapel. A memorial built on the site of the fire. But yes, I walked."

"And you're sure you feel safe?"

"I'm totally fine." She didn't tell him about the men loitering near the hotel last night or the teenagers who'd approached her asking for money on her walk to the chapel this morning. He would only worry, and she was being cautious and aware of her surroundings. She scrambled for something to change the subject again. "I'm getting my exercise with all the walking I'm doing, that's for sure."

"Okay. Well, I'll let you get back to your research. Have fun."

"Thanks, honey. I am. Is everything going okay there?"

"Other than a demanding guest. And Alex sleeping on my face."

She laughed. "Oh, I miss Alex. Give him a hug for me." Somewhere in the city a church bell chimed the hour. "I probably need to go, honey. I'll talk to you soon."

"Be safe, love."

She clicked End and slid her phone into the inside pocket of her purse, feeling strangely empty. She couldn't remember ever having such awkward conversations with Arthur Tyler. It might have been easier if they'd agreed not to talk until she returned home. But what did that say about the state of their marriage?

With that question nagging at the back of her mind, she went back inside the chapel.

Eight

Art plugged his phone back into the charger. Not that he'd talked to Maddie long enough to run down his battery. It sounded like she missed Alex more than she missed him. And it sounded like she was awfully anxious to get off the phone.

A heaviness settled over his shoulders. And his task for today was not going to lighten his burden. He'd promised Maddie he would visit her mom in the nursing home once a week while Maddie was away. He often went with her when she visited Mildred, but he counted on her to prompt the conversation—which tended to be rather one-sided. Hmm...not unlike his conversations with Maddie recently.

He went to start the coffeemaker and pull one of Maddie's breakfast casseroles out of the freezer to thaw. There was only one couple to feed this morning, but they were checking out early and requested breakfast at seven. He would get the laundry going after they left, then go see Mildred. Maybe he would stop by Ginny's house, too, before he headed back home. After all, Maddie wasn't the only woman in his life.

He snorted at his own attempt at a joke. But he felt a little better just thinking of doing something he knew would make someone else happy. He'd done enough moping.

At ten o'clock, with his guests gone, breakfast dishes drying on the counter, and Alex fed, Art grabbed his jacket and cap off the hook by the back door and headed for town.

On a whim, he stopped at Clayburn's little flower shop downtown. It would make Maddie happy to know that he'd bought flowers for her mom. Maizie Callahan, who'd owned the flower shop as long as he could remember, greeted him with a smile that quickly faded. "Uh-oh. You look like a man in need of make-up flowers."

He gave her a quizzical look.

"Valentine's Day has passed, and if I recall, Maddie's birthday is in the summer."

He feigned a stern look. "Does a man need a reason to bring his wife flowers?"

"Ooh, good answer, Arthur Tyler." She arched a penciled eyebrow.

He laughed. "Actually, Maddie is away on a research trip. I thought I'd take some flowers to her mom at the nursing home."

"You sweet man!"

Art laughed again. "What do you have that won't break the bank?"

Now it was Maizie's turn to laugh. "Now there's the Art I know." She turned to the walk-in cooler that held buckets of colorful blooms. "Carnations are always going to be your best buy. Or daisies when they're in season. Of course, the ladies in town all know those are the cheap buys. If you want to give something extra special, go with tulips. A little pricier to be sure, but you won't find a more delightful offering for the ladies in your life. Especially this time of year when everyone is longing for spring."

Art shook his head slowly. "You should have gone into sales, Maizie."

She gave him a smug, tongue-in-cheek look. "Tulips then?"

"Tulips it is." He fished his wallet out of his back pocket. "And you know what? Make it two bundles—or bunches or whatever you call them."

"Bouquets, you mean?"

"Yes, that's it. But can you just put them in vases without arranging them?"

"Two vases?" Maizie looked confused.

"That's how Maddie prefers her flowers," he explained. "Like she picked them fresh out of the garden herself."

"But I thought you said Maddie was on a research trip. Tulips don't have a very long vase life. When does she get home?"

"Oh, these aren't for Maddie."

"I see." She waited expectantly.

But he didn't give her the satisfaction.

"Two vases of tulips," Maizie finally said. "We can do that. Just be sure to add more water when you get to the nursing home...or *wherever* you're taking them."

It was all Art could do not to laugh out loud. But he didn't, nor did he answer Maizie's veiled question. This town could use a little imaginary scandal. Let the rumors fly.

Ten minutes later he drove carefully to the nursing home, two vases of tulips riding precariously in the cupholders in the console. He took a parking place close to the entrance, grabbed one of the vases, and said a little prayer that Maddie's mom was having a good day.

His face warmed when the two nurse aides at the front desk made a fuss over his "sweeter than pie" gesture of bringing flowers. He escaped down the hall, thankful Mildred's door was ajar. He ducked into her room and closed the door behind him.

She looked up and her eyes brightened when they landed on the bouquet. "Tiptoes."

He gave her a quizzical look, and then it hit him. "Ah... Tiptoe through the tulips, huh?"

She nodded. "Tiptoes."

"I need to get some more water for these, okay?"

"Okay?" she parroted.

He went into the small ensuite bathroom and tried to fit the vase under the faucet but only managed to spill out most of the water that was already in the vase.

"I'll be right back, Mildred." He explained where he was going even though her blank stare said she didn't understand a word of it.

A quick trip to the water fountain down the hall and he was back to set the vase on the table beside Mildred's chair. He made a mental note to put the glass vase up high before he left, where it wouldn't be in danger of getting broken.

He pulled a chair up close to hers and sat down, putting a hand over hers on her lap. She looked up at him expectantly.

"Maddie said to tell you hello. She's on a research trip right now but she'll be back soon."

Nothing. Back to a vacant stare. No indication she understood what he'd said or was even aware he was speaking to her. How hard it must be for Maddie to see her mother like this. To try to carry a conversation. But maybe she didn't try.

He remembered Maddie saying that she sometimes read to her mom. Maybe he could go that route. He glanced around the room for a book, but finding only a few women's magazines, he pulled up his Bible app on his phone. He hadn't read more than a few verses since Maddie left, so he could kill two birds with one stone this way.

Feeling bad he'd come up with that particular adage in reference to Maddie's mom, he patted her hand in silent apology. "How about some Psalms, Mildred?"

Again, no response he could discern. But he began to read anyway. He read from the first Psalm to the end of the twenty-second. Looking ahead, he recognized the "funeral" Psalm and decided it might be good to avoid the valley of the shadow of death. This would be a good place to stop. Besides, he still had another flower delivery to make.

He tucked his phone back in his hip pocket and looked up to

see that Mildred had fallen asleep in her chair. He smiled and whispered, "Didn't know I was that boring."

She opened her eyes at that and gave him a little smile. He patted her hand again. "You go ahead and get some rest, Mildred. I need to get going. But I'll see you again soon, okay?"

She didn't reply but watched him as he rose and set the vase of flowers on a doily on top of her tallboy dresser.

"Maddie sends her love."

He backed out of the room with an anemic wave and was glad to find the nurses' station empty.

When he reached his car, he was surprised to realize he'd only been inside for forty-five minutes. It had seemed like an eternity. Even so, he was glad he'd gone. And it would give him something positive to tell Maddie next time they talked. Of course, who knew when that might be?

The heaviness returned. This being five thousand miles away from her was the pits! How he longed for the days when he would come home to find her—and a savory supper—waiting for him. Or even the days before that when their love was just blossoming and she was a quickly-penned note away.

But wait... Wasn't she still? Even an ocean away? After all, they lived in a digital world. An idea started to take shape, and the more the details arranged themselves in his brain, the lighter he felt.

He would ask Ginny what she thought of his idea, but he felt sure she would approve.

By the time she arrived back at the hotel, Maddie's feet were throbbing. According to her phone, she'd walked nearly ten miles today! But oh, the material she'd gathered for her books. How had she ever thought she could write this series without spending time in Paris?

She made a mental note to start saving for a trip back here

next year when she would be starting the second novel. And maybe next time, they could wait until spring break when Art could come with her. They couldn't be cross with each other in this magical place, could they?

The automatic doors slid open and she crossed the lobby toward the front desk to pick up her key. Two young women were unwrapping takeout in the dining room next to the lobby and the savory aroma wafted under her nose. Her stomach growled, reminding her that since breakfast at the hotel, she hadn't eaten more than a small grilled eggplant falafel and a gelato from a street vendor. Maybe she would order in tonight though. Her feet needed a break.

Monsieur Bajwa was at the desk again and she instinctively felt in the side pocket of her purse for her phone, still embarrassed she'd left it behind her first day in the city.

Monsieur Bajwa reached into the drawer under the counter and produced the key to Room 104. But when she reached to take it from him, he drew it back with a grin that said he knew exactly what she was thinking. "You will take care of your key, oui, Madame?"

"I promise." She laughed and patted her purse. "And my phone is safe with me as well."

She climbed the curved staircase to her room. She couldn't wait to soak her feet in the tub and change into comfy clothes. Minutes later, she curled up on the bed with her laptop. Feeling herself grow drowsy, she set an alarm so she wouldn't fall asleep and worry Art again.

As if she'd summoned him with her thoughts, a text from Art appeared in the corner of her laptop screen.

—*How was the rest of your day?*

—*SO good. I don't know how I thought I could write this book without coming here.*

—*I'm glad. I went to see your mom today.*

She was touched that he'd gone to visit so soon. She scooted upright in the bed and typed a reply.

*—Aww, thanks for going. How was she?*

*—About the same. She perked up a couple of times, but was mostly quiet. We read some psalms.*

She pictured her handsome husband sitting beside Mom, reading to her from the Bible, and her heart warmed.

*—I love you, Arthur Tyler.*

A smiley face with hearts surrounding it appeared on her screen. Maddie laughed. Art was the least likely to use an emoji of anyone she knew. A desperate longing for him came over her. She tapped out quickly:

*—Can I call you?*

A long pause and then:

*—True confession: I'm sitting in a faculty meeting. Back of the room. It'll probably go long. Boring stuff.*

*—Ah, discussing popular fiction, huh?*

But she quickly deleted it. Might be too soon to joke about that. And too easily misunderstood in a text. But it made her giggle. And gave her hope that someday they'd be able to laugh about this.

Instead, she typed:

*—I'd better let you go. I can't keep my eyes open anyway.*

*—Maybe tomorrow?*

She echoed his text:

*—Maybe tomorrow.*

Then she clicked off, feeling a strange dichotomy of hope and sadness. Why had she made such a mess of things before she left? And now, with an ocean separating them and their clocks in constant conflict, it seemed as if they'd never find time to sort things out.

Nine

Maddie was glad she'd skipped the Louvre today, grand though it was. Thankfully, she'd spent hours at the art museum eight years ago and her research this time around was more important—and quickly coming to an end after two busy days in Paris. The idyllic neighborhoods she'd explored near the chapel of Notre-Dame-de-Consolation were like gold. Ideas were overflowing. Good thing, since tomorrow afternoon the whirlwind of book signings and book club appearances would begin.

On her way back to the hotel, she left the bustling street and dropped down to river level via the stone steps that led to the wide sidewalks alongside the Seine. A few boats floated lazily on the water and its fishy odor mingled with the pungent scent of cherry blossoms opening. As bees and butterflies flitted among the branches collecting nectar, butterflies of a different sort assaulted her as she thought about tomorrow's event.

She'd told Art she'd have an "escort" once the events began, but it seemed she and Janice had a little different definition of the word. She had a contact or host once she arrived at each event, but not one person who would arrange transportation for the events. She was on her own there, which was fine with her, but she knew Art would not be happy about the turn of events.

She'd done dozens of book signings in the years since her first novel was published, but never one where she worried about how she might communicate with the readers attending. A nerve-wracking thought struck her: What if she didn't know how to spell the uniquely French names of the patrons she signed books for? Maybe she should have them write their names on a slip of paper so she could copy from that. She'd seen that done at a few book signings of famous authors with long lines wrapped around the building. At least she wouldn't have to worry about that "problem."

Of course, one of Janice's French-speaking American friends would be there to help with the language barrier. She'd talked with her editor on the phone this morning, and Janice assured her everyone was most eager for her visits.

Her first event tomorrow was late afternoon at a tiny book-shop near Montmartre in the 18th arrondissement. It was about an hour's walk from the hotel, but unless it was raining, she planned to leave early and walk to the beautiful Sacré Coeur cathedral and spend some time there and in Montmartre before her signing. She could carry her stylish shoes and a dressier jacket in her backpack and freshen up at the bookstore before her event started. Then, because it would likely be dark when she was finished, she would take a cab back.

She walked past a boulangerie and breathed in the buttery scent of fresh croissants and baguettes, then passed by a sidewalk macaron vendor who'd parked his charming cart under a bower of cherry buds on the verge of bursting into bloom. She went back and bought a small box of the colorful cookies and snapped some photos. Janice had already chided her once about not posting anything about her research trip online yet. She'd made a mental note to take lots of photos at the signing tonight, but this would make a cute post in the meantime, even though it wasn't exactly about books.

The vendor pointed to her phone and beckoned her. "I take photo of you, Madame?"

She started to decline, but it would be nice to have at least a few photos with her in them. "Merci!" She handed him her phone.

To her surprise, he stepped around in front of the cart and motioned for her to pose beside it. She tried to look pleasant. He looked at the screen, then at her. He frowned, then pushed up one side of his mouth with his index finger. "Le sourire! A smile for the camera, non?"

Feeling awkward, she obliged him. He took several shots, but on checking the screen, he shook his head, apparently not satisfied with the results. He danced a silly jig that made her laugh.

He quickly snapped again. "Ah, oui! Beaucoup mieux!"

Still laughing, she took the camera back from him. "Merci beaucoup, Monsieur."

Well, that was done. How these influencers filmed themselves all day long, she would never know. But it was a small courtesy she could offer Janice, who'd arranged this entire trip for her. She wished there was a way to ship a package of macarons to New York before they went stale—or arrived as a pile of confetti-like crumbs—but there was still time to find a fun little thank-you gift to send the publishing team.

She put her phone away, adjusted her crossbody bag, and started toward the hotel again. Despite not having walked nearly as far today, her feet didn't hurt any less, and she was happy when the alley entrance to the Rue Jean Lantier came into view. Already, her little neighborhood felt familiar and exponentially safer than it had that first night she'd arrived.

She breezed through the sliding doors and headed for the front desk to pick up her key. Monsieur Bajwa wasn't at his usual spot behind the desk, but an Indian woman wearing a traditional kurti and matching scarf retrieved her key from the drawer after Maddie gave her room number.

Maddie had seen the young woman there before and wondered if she might be Monsieur Bajwa's wife. "Bonsoir."

"Merci. À vous aussi." Maddie rounded the corner to climb the stairs when she heard her name.

"Ah! Madame Houser?"

Maddie reversed her direction and caught the eye of the woman again.

"Excusez-moi, I just remembered. You are Madame Houser, non? There is a delivery for you."

"Oh?" Probably something from Janice.

The woman disappeared into a curtained doorway behind the registration desk and returned, smiling, with a gorgeous bouquet of tulips in a glass vase. "For you."

"How lovely," she whispered. "Merci." There was a card in a tiny envelope tucked into the bouquet, but she would wait until she was back in her room before she read it.

Maybe Janice had sent them, but she supposed it could also be the bookshop. They wouldn't have wanted her to have to carry such a large bouquet back to the hotel.

She shifted her belongings to accommodate the bouquet, thanked the woman again, and climbed the stairs to her room. A fresh, springy scent wafted up from the colorful tulips. It would be a treat to have flowers in her room for the next few days. But goodness! If every place she had a signing sent flowers... She smiled at the thought.

In her room, she put her things away, then opened the little card that came with the bouquet.

I KNOW YOU ARE WHERE YOU'RE SUPPOSED TO BE, BUT I FEEL LIKE A PIECE OF MY HEART IS MISSING. HURRY BACK TO ME, LOVE. *Art*

Tears came hard and fast, surprising her. He *did* miss her. And him saying a piece of his heart was missing because she was away? That meant more than a thousand I-love-yous. Even as her husband's sweet words soothed and healed, they also cut deeply because she didn't deserve them. Didn't deserve *him*. She'd let petty issues turn into mountains. And then she'd as good as run away from home instead of staying and working things out.

She sank onto the bed and buried her face in the pillows. "Oh, Lord... Please give me another chance. Please let me get safely home to him and make things right between us."

Suddenly, the two and a half weeks she had left in Paris seemed an eternity.

Art stopped at the grocery store on the way home from his afternoon class. He had guests again tonight and needed fresh fruit to go with the coffee cake Maddie had left in the freezer.

An endcap display near the produce section overflowed with flowers. He looked at the price sticker on a sleeve of tulips and rolled his eyes. He could have saved a small fortune on the flowers for Ginny and Maddie's mom. But then, if he hadn't gone to the flower shop, he probably wouldn't have thought to order tulips from a Parisian florist for Maddie. And something about that small gift—along with his sappy, but heartfelt message—had lifted his own spirits. Maybe it was merely the aggregate of sending flowers to three women in one day. The Lord above knew he could not afford to do so *every* week. But this week anyway, the nearly two hundred dollars he'd dropped on three dozen tulips felt like money well spent. And as a nice bonus, Ginny's flowers had resulted in an invitation to her house for supper.

Although he had a sneaking suspicion Ginny had ulterior motives for inviting him. The sweet octogenarian would always have a special place in his and Maddie's hearts because of her role in bringing them together, but there was something unsettling about the way the woman could read his demeanor and moods.

When he'd delivered the bouquet to Ginny yesterday, she'd given him a searching look and asked if everything was okay. He hadn't exactly been lying when he told her all was well. But then when he explained about Maddie's book tour in Paris, he thought her expression turned to disapproval. He tried to defend Maddie, explaining about the research she needed to do in order to fulfill her contract. He knew Ginny loved Maddie's books. Annie had shared her copies with the older woman. But he imagined that Ginny was of the mindset that married women shouldn't work, although he thought she'd mentioned working in her younger days even after she was married.

He brushed aside the thoughts and added a carton of strawberries and one of blueberries to his grocery cart.

He got some ice cream for a treat later tonight. Alex would appreciate that. As he pushed his cart toward the checkout line, his phone dinged with a text.

*—You are the sweetest man on earth. Merci beaucoup!*

He smiled. Mission accomplished. He secured a place in the shortest checkout line before replying.

*—I take it you got my roses. :)*

A rather long pause followed. Then another ding.

*—Oh, honey...they were tulips! But that's even better. I LOVE tulips.*

*—I know, silly. I was just teasing you. Glad you like them.*

*—They are gorgeous. I can't believe you thought to do that.*

*—Well, actually, you can thank your mom. And Maizie.*

*—What? Not following.*

*—I drove by the flower shop and had the idea to take flowers to your mom. Maizie suggested tulips and there was a discount if you bought two bouquets, so I took one to Ginny too. And then I found myself wishing I could get you one. And then it struck me that DUH, I could!*

*—Oh, you darling man! It's even sweeter that you took flowers to Mom and Ginny. I bet they loved them.*

*—So much that I have an invitation to supper at Ginny's next Thursday.*

*—LOL! You're a tricky one!*

*—Did you have a good day?*

*—Très bonne. But I miss you.*

*—I don't know what "tray bone" means, but I miss you too.*

Laughing at his own joke, he pushed his cart forward and put his groceries on the conveyor.

*—I'm next in line at Kroger. I'd better go. I love you. Knock 'em dead tomorrow!*

A little heart appeared on his message. Then another ding just as the customer in front of him wheeled her cart away. He checked his screen to find a photo of Maddie standing on a cobbled street under some pink blossoms. She looked stylish and gorgeous. And yet the smile she wore didn't quite reach her eyes. Not the genuine beam of sunshine he knew and loved.

And he dared to hope he was to blame.

He hearted her photo and put his phone back in his pocket.

Ten

The cozy bookshop was redolent of musty books, aging roses, and steaming tea with milk and honey. Everything Maddie had dreamed a French bookstore would be. Little lamps and candles flickered from various shelves, and the room buzzed with a pleasant mixture of French and English— English that, to Maddie's ears, had never sounded less like her native language.

Two dozen women, most of them closer to Ginny's age than her own, had already gathered by the time Maddie arrived, and as she spoke, they seemed enthralled with tales of how her novels had come to be, how she'd ended up here in Paris writing about the tragic fire at the Bazar de la Charité, and especially with her descriptions of life in rural Kansas. Several expressed interest in visiting Annabeth's Inn the next time they were in the States. She had a feeling they had no idea how far Kansas was from New York or Los Angeles.

Despite the comfortable Louis IV chair they offered her when it was time to sign books, she was exhausted from a day spent exploring the Musée d'Orsay, then walking the longer than expected distance to the bookshop, and now, with listening so carefully to understand each person who came to her with a book to sign. Even so, she felt like the evening had gone splendidly.

The French women who'd come to hear her were altogether gracious and *très* patient with her horrid French. She sold a decent number of books as well, although Janice had assured her this book tour wasn't about sales as much as it was about gaining new readers for the French translations of her novels that would hopefully soon be available all over the country and in other French-speaking countries, including the province of Quebec, Canada.

During a pause in the conversation, her hostess, Gisèle, the bookstore manager, touched her shoulder. "Could I get you another cup of tea, Madame Houser?"

"Oh, please, call me Maddie... S'il vous plaît," she added quickly. She'd done her best to use as much French as she could muster, but as Janice predicted, the women seemed content to practice their English with her. "And oui, I would love more tea. Merci."

A few minutes later, a steaming cup was set before her. She sipped slowly, savoring its subtle lavender aroma. It was her third cup of the brew since she'd arrived. She'd have to remember to use the restroom before she caught a cab back to the hotel. Right now the hotel sounded good.

Closing time came and went, and after Gisèle practically shooed away the last customer, she turned to Maddie with a satisfied smile. "What a delightful evening. They loved you, Maddie!"

"Oh...do you really think so? I just hope they could understand me."

"Of course they could. Your English is perfect."

Maddie laughed. "I wasn't so worried about my English. It's my French that's très rusty."

"Ah bien, they loved you, rust and all. We even sold a few books."

"Well, I hope you'll sell more than a few when the translations are finished."

"Oui, I have no doubt! You'll have to return to us then."

"I'd love that." Maddie started to fold up one of the vintage wooden folding chairs the women had been seated on.

"Non!" Gisèle clicked her tongue and took the chair from her. "You are our guest. My girls will take care of that. We need to get you home."

"Merci. I *am* exhausted."

"But of course you are. Come!" Gisèle motioned toward the back room where Maddie had stored her purse and the backpack with her walking shoes and her change of clothes. "I'll drive you."

"Oh, you don't need to do that. I can call a cab."

"A taxi? Nonsense! You're staying in the 1st arrondissement, non? That's practically on my way home."

"Merci. You are too kind."

Gisèle drove expertly through the city streets, and Maddie relished the sparkling views of Paris at night through her open window. One neighborhood gave way to another, and soon the panorama outside her window began to look familiar. "I'm right up here on the left." Maddie instructed Gisèle to drop her off where the taxi had her first day in the city.

"This ruelle? But where is your hotel? I will take you there."

Maddie laughed. Even this Parisian thought it was an alley, not a street. "The hotel is just a short walk up the alley."

"There's surely a closer place to drop you? I will walk you to the door." Gisèle cut the engine.

"Nonsense!" Maddie smiled at how much she sounded like her host. "Truly, Gisèle, there's no need. It's not even a minute's walk. You might get a parking ticket. And besides, then who would escort *you* back to your car?"

"Well, you do make a point... If you're certain."

"Absolutely. Thank you so much for a lovely evening."

"Ah, the pleasure was all ours. Bonne nuit. Till we meet again."

Maddie got out and gave a little wave. Gisèle blew a kiss across the top of the car and climbed back in.

Maddie sighed with contentment. It seemed like she'd been in

Paris for weeks, not a mere three days. But tonight, her heart was full. She could report to Janice that her first event had gone swimmingly, and she could report to Art that she'd made a friend.

She hurried down the alley, keeping to the middle, away from the dark, narrow crevices between buildings. She hadn't been out here after dark before, and although she recognized the light from the hotel entrance spilling onto the path ahead of her, it was darker in the alley with the buildings blocking the city lights.

She quickened her pace when she saw two men loitering across from the hotel. Maybe the same two young men who'd been here smoking that first night she arrived. When they saw her, they put their heads together, whispering. She walked faster.

"Mademoiselle!" They sauntered toward her, one of them saying something to her in French. She couldn't understand his words, but she knew the seductive tone. Her pulse quickened and her throat went dry.

The hotel was only three or four car lengths in front of her on her left. She shook her head pointedly at them. "Je ne parle pas Français."

She veered to the other side of the street, forcing herself not to run as she got closer to the door.

They kept advancing toward her. The taller man, just a kid really—maybe seventeen or eighteen—said something to the other.

Then, without warning, they rushed her, grabbing for her bags.

She screamed at the top of her lungs and clawed at them like a frightened kitten. Remembering her valuables in her crossbody bag, she clung to it with all her strength. But even as she did, she felt her backpack being ripped off her shoulder. With a shout, the taller man ran off with it. But the other one gripped the strap of her crossbody bag and almost pulled her down with it. She screamed again, her heart pounding, her mind racing. She could *not* lose her bag!

Someone shouted from the doorway of the hotel and the man instantly let go of her bag and high-tailed it down the alley.

Maddie looked up to see Monsieur Bajwa shaking his fist at the men before they disappeared between the buildings. "Vagabonds!" He rushed to Maddie's side. "Are you injured, Madame?"

Panting and trembling like a leaf in the Kansas wind, she tried to ascertain if she was in one piece. She clasped her bag closer to her chest. At least they hadn't gotten that.

"Did they rob you, Ma'am?"

"They—" She couldn't make her voice work right. "They took my backpack."

"Voleurs! Your valuables?" He looked pointedly at the cross-body bag she still clutched.

Her reply came out in a giggle that made her sound a little demented. "Just my stinky walking shoes and my other clothes."

The woman Maddie assumed was Monsieur Bajwa's wife appeared beside her. She put a hand on Maddie's arm. "Come inside. I get you something to drink. You are unhurt?"

"I...I think so. Thank you. Merci," she corrected quickly.

"Was there anything else in the rucksack?" he asked.

She thought for a moment. "Nothing important. My umbrella. Some chocolates and bookmarks they gave me at the bookstore. Some brochures. Nothing of real value." She was beyond grateful that she'd cleaned out her backpack before she left for the event tonight.

"You will buy new shoes tomorrow, non?"

"Oh, I have another pair that will work. In my luggage. There was nothing truly important in the bag. It...it could have been so much worse."

"You come inside now." The woman took her arm and led her toward the hotel's entrance.

Once they were in the lobby, Monsieur Bajwa barked an order at the woman in a way that convinced Maddie she was, indeed, his wife.

He went to the desk, retrieved her key, and laid it carefully on the bar counter in front of Maddie. Madame Bajwa went behind the little bar beside the registration desk and pulled a bottle of amber liquid—whiskey, maybe?—from the shelf. She picked up a tumbler and gave Maddie a questioning look.

Maddie put up a hand. "Oh no. Just water, please. S'il vous plaît," she added, remembering her manners.

The woman shook her head disapprovingly but took a bottle of water from a small fridge and poured the tumbler half full. "You sit." She motioned to a bar stool.

"Merci. Thank you so much." Suddenly, near tears, Maddie slumped onto the stool. It could have been *so* much worse. But now, she would have to tell Art what had happened. After all his warnings.

Monsieur Bajwa came and stood beside his wife. He spoke softly to Maddie. "In the future, if you return after dark, you insist the driver comes in the other way. Via Rue Bertin Poirée." He pointed in the direction of the breakfast room, and Maddie remembered seeing where Rue Jean Lantier dead-ended in that direction at a street opposite where the taxi and Gisèle had dropped her off.

"Thank you. I will." She finished the water in the tumbler and took the bottle of water, sliding off the stool. "I'm going up to my room now. Thank you for your help."

"Bonne nuit," the Bajwas said in unison.

She started toward the stairway, then turned back. "Has this... happened before?"

They both shook their heads adamantly. "Rarely, but I will inform la police so they are aware. You are safe here, Madame, I assure you."

"Thank you. Merci. I don't know what would have happened if you hadn't come when you did."

He gave a graceful little bow before sliding back behind the desk.

She climbed the curve of the stairs, key in hand but found she could hardly fit it in the keyhole because her hands were trembling so. She had to get hold of herself before she called Art.

189

*Eleven*

"Now that we got the chitchat out of the way, tell me why you're really here, Arthur." Ginny stared at him with dogged determination in her eyes.

"What do you mean…'really here?' I just wanted to stop by and see how you were doing. And thank you for the invitation to supper next week."

"Hogwash." She shook her gray head and nodded toward the vase of tulips in the center of her dining room table. "When you brought me these pretty tulips—which I've enjoyed immensely, by the way—you just wanted to stop by and see how I was doing. I assure you I haven't deteriorated much in seventy-two hours. There's something troubling you, and I'm not letting you out of here until you tell me what it is."

He cocked his head. "How do you do that?"

Unlike him, she didn't pretend to be ignorant of what he was talking about. "I was married for almost half a century, young man. I know a domestic storm brewing when I see one."

He slumped back in the rocking chair Ginny had offered ten minutes ago. "I don't even know how to describe what's going on."

"Maybe you're just missing your bride, dear. Could it be that simple? Three weeks is a long time to be apart when you're young and in love."

He shook his head, too weary to keep up with a ruse any longer. "It's more than that. I'm afraid I've really messed up, Ginny."

"Do you want to talk about it?"

He combed his fingers through his hair. "I thought I'd worked through everything—with Annie—before Maddie and I got married. I felt such peace about it on our wedding day. But I guess...I've backslidden. It's going on three years, Ginny, and sometimes the grief feels as fresh as that first year."

"Ah... April. The anniversary is coming up. Spring will probably always be a little bittersweet for you. That's perfectly understandable, Art. Talk to Maddie. Does she know that anniversary is coming up?"

"I told her Annie died in April. But I don't know if she remembers."

"Then tell her again. Gently, of course. But if I know Maddie, she'll be sympathetic."

He shook his head. "She's been nothing but kind toward Annie. Her memory, I mean. The worst thing is...I can't seem to quit comparing them."

"With Maddie coming up short, I'm guessing."

"Sometimes," he admitted. "I love Maddie. I do. But things are...different. This marriage. *She's* different."

"Well, of course she is. God didn't make any of us the same—and thank goodness for that."

"It's just hard to get used to. I know Maddie's adjusting to things too. She was on her own for a long time. She keeps reminding me that she's a big girl and she can do things without me."

Ginny chuckled. "And I know our Annie wasn't like that, was she? She had a more timid nature. And I imagine you liked the fact that she needed you and always wanted to be with you."

He thought for a moment. "I guess I did. Not that Annie was needy. She wasn't."

"I'm not saying that either. She was just happy to go along with whatever you wanted to do, wherever you wanted to go."

"She was." He nodded. "I hope she wasn't just...faking it. I did ask her opinion. Especially after she got sick. I didn't want her to die with any regrets. But she always just said, 'Whatever you want, Art.'"

"I assure you, our dear Annie wasn't faking it. That was just her personality. And, Art..." She patted his hand across the little table that held their empty teacups. "You don't ever need to worry that Annie wasn't happy with you. She was supremely happy. She told me that almost every time I saw her. Don't ever let anyone tell you otherwise."

"I called Maddie by Annie's name a few weeks ago." He blurted it out, feeling relieved to have confessed.

"Ahh..." Ginny nodded matter-of-factly. "And how did that go over?"

He gave a dry laugh. "Not very well."

"I would imagine not. But that's bound to happen. You and Annie were married for nearly a decade. And I'm sure it doesn't help that their names are only a few letters apart. So how did Maddie react?"

"Well, we were already in a fight. And my thoughtlessness didn't help matters any, let me tell you."

She said nothing for a moment. "Have you asked for forgiveness? Maddie doesn't seem like one to hold a grudge."

"She said she's forgiven me. But what if I do it again? Ever since that happened—and I saw how much it hurt her—I feel like I'm walking on pins and needles for fear I'll do it again."

"And maybe you will. Old habits die hard. But I hope she realizes that, in a way, it's a compliment—that when you're with Maddie, you feel those same feelings of love you had for Annie."

He huffed and shot her a grin. "I wish I'd thought of that when it happened."

She winked. "You can put that in your back pocket in case it happens again. You're welcome."

His laughter faded. "It's just that when I lost Annie, I—"

"Whoa. Whoa, stop right there." Ginny held up a wrinkled hand. "Sweet man, you didn't *lose* Annie. You know exactly where she is. She's home. She's where God intended all along for her to be for eternity. Yes, it happened too soon. And it *feels* like a loss. Of course it does because, as God also intended, the two of you became one. But if you'll remember your wedding vows, same as with Maddie, you promised till death do you part. Well, that happened, Art. Death parted you. It was tragic and sad and heartbreaking and all the adjectives and adverbs. I'm sure in your profession you have buckets more of those than I do." The glimmer in her eyes held humor...and compassion. "But bottom line, it was devastating. Here's the thing, Art. You fulfilled every promise you made to that woman. I know for a fact that she died thinking you were a saint. And I also know for a fact that she's been set straight on that account by now."

He couldn't help but smile.

"I think, dear Art, that you got stuck in a downward spiral after Annie died. You assumed you could never be happy again and now that God has put another wonderful woman in your life, you're afraid to let go of Annie and simply enjoy Maddie as the gift from God that she is. The unique, one-of-a-kind, very-different-from-Annie gift from God. But still a gift made just for you." Ginny reached over and patted his knee. "Let go, Art! Oh not of memories of Annie. You'll carry those with you until the day you die. And truthfully, in a way, Maddie owes a debt of gratitude to Annie. Because God used your precious Annie to make you the man you are today." She sighed. "All that to say... Receive the gift God gave you. Enjoy Maddie to the fullest. Without guilt."

He frowned. "I know you're right, but that's a little hard to do when she's in France and I'm in Clayburn."

"Do you think Maddie was running away when she planned

her trip? She does intend to come back, right?" Ginny looked genuinely worried.

"She's coming back. We promised till death do us part, but... Those promises feel far more...fragile than they did the day we spoke them."

"Ah, Art. One thing I know about Maddie is that she keeps her word." She gave a definitive nod of her chin. "Maybe this time apart will give you both a chance to think things through. See things a little clearer."

"Maybe. It's just a long time, three weeks. And with the time difference, it's like we're living in completely different worlds. When she calls, she's always rushing off to somewhere. I mean, it's not like we're arguing or anything, but there's just such a distance between us. It's like we don't even speak the same language any more."

"You know, I remember when Grover was working construction and he'd be gone for long stretches—though never as long as three weeks." She clucked her tongue. "When he'd come home, for the first day or so, we felt like strangers to each other. But it never lasted for long. Soon, we'd get used to each other once more, and before you knew it, everything felt right again. Or at least—"

Art's phone vibrated loudly in his pocket. "Sorry, Ginny." He checked the screen. "Oh, it's Maddie. I'd better take—"

"Take it!" Ginny rose from the table and shooed him away like she would've a pesky mosquito. "Give her my love."

He checked his watch and was alarmed to realize it was after midnight in Paris. "It's late over there."

Ginny waved him off and busied herself stacking their cups and saucers at the table.

Art clicked Accept. "Maddie? Hey, is everything okay?"

For a moment there was only silence and he wondered if he was talking to the Indian man at the hotel again.

Finally Maddie's voice came across the line. "Hi honey."

"Maddie? You're up awfully late. Is everything okay?"

A muffled sob and then she was speaking almost incoherently. The few words he caught didn't reassure him. "Maddie, slow down. Are you all right?"

"I'm okay. Don't worry. I'm sorry... I thought I had it together before I dialed but—"

"Tell me what happened. Are you in a safe place?"

"I'm fine." She gave a nervous laugh. "I'm fine, honey, really. I had a little incident outside the hotel, but everything is okay. I didn't mean to crumble like that."

"Incident? What happened?"

"Oh, some stupid kids tried to take my purse."

"You were mugged? Maddie!"

"I'm fine, Art. They didn't take anything important."

"What? But what *did* they take?"

Again, that nervous laughter. "Only my backpack."

"Wait. They *stole* your backpack? While you were carrying it?" *What on earth?*

"Thank the Lord, I'd cleaned it out before I left for the signing." She blew a sigh into the phone. "It only had my walking shoes and my umbrella, some things the bookstore gave me. Nothing I can't live without at all. I will miss my backpack though."

"Are you saying they forcefully took your backpack from you?"

"Yes," she squeaked. "They tried to grab my purse, too, but thankfully, the guy at the hotel came out and chased them off."

"They attacked you? Maddie, what in the world—?"

"It was just some teenagers, Art. They didn't hurt me."

"I don't care. They could have!" He struggled to keep his tone even. "Where did it happen? You must have been terrified."

"It was...a little scary." The words tumbled out of her now as she laid out the details of a mugging right in front of her hotel. "So that's the gist of it. I'm just thankful for Monsieur Bajwa and his wife."

"Who's that? Maddie that hotel doesn't sound like a safe place for you to be!"

"Monsieur Bajwa and his wife manage the hotel. They heard the commotion and came out and chased the kids away."

"You're sure you're okay? Where are you now? Maybe you should have a doctor check you over. When did this happen?"

She laughed again, but sounded more like herself this time. "I'm perfectly fine, Art. Just a little shook up is all. They didn't hurt me."

"When did it happen?" he asked again.

"I don't know... I guess about an hour ago?"

"You're not going to stay there are you?"

"At the hotel? It's perfectly safe, honey. It was a fluke. It's not like they were trying to kill me."

"It doesn't sound perfectly safe to me."

At that, Ginny looked up her forehead furrowed, her gray head shaking. Art was aware she'd been praying.

He met Ginny's eyes. "Maddie, I really wish you'd change hotels. Just put it on our card. I don't care what Janice says."

"Art, I— I'll think about it, honey. But I truly think this is a very safe part of the city. The Bajwas are taking good care of me."

He huffed. "I don't know about that."

"Monsieur Bajwa told me where to have drivers drop me off so I don't have to walk down the alley again."

"Alley? Where are you now? I do not like the sound of this *at all*."

"I'm in my room at the hotel. I'll explain everything when I get home. But I promise you everything is fine. I just didn't want you to hear about it online or something."

"It was on the news?" His voice rose out of control. This just got worse and worse.

Ginny gave him a questioning look and clucked her tongue in disapproval.

"No. Not that I know of. But you never know. I just thought

in case you googled the hotel or something and saw there'd been an incident."

"Were the police called?"

"No. They have better things to do than chase down my stinky shoes."

He inhaled deeply and scrubbed his face with his hands, feeling utterly helpless. "Listen, love, if you're sure you're safe in your room, then you need to get some sleep. It's late there and you have events tomorrow, don't you?"

"Not until après-midi."

"English, please."

She gave a hollow laugh. "Sorry. Afternoon. After lunch. I'm trying to use my French, such as it is, as much as possible while I'm here."

She was sounding more like herself, but that was little comfort. "I wish you'd consider changing hotels."

"Art, please don't worry about me. It could have happened anywhere. I promise I'm fine. I'm sorry I cried. I thought I had my emotions under control, but when I heard your voice I just kind of...lost it."

He glanced at Ginny, who'd gone back to praying. He slid out of his chair and went into the living room, wanting to say things to Maddie that felt too personal, too intimate. "I miss you," he whispered. "Let's never do this again, okay?"

"Do what?"

"Be so far apart. For so long. I don't like it."

"I know. I don't either. We should have—" Her voice broke and she started again. "*I* should never have agreed to come without you."

"Shh. We'll talk when you get home. Just be careful. Come home to me."

"That's my plan."

He hung up aching for her.

He found Ginny at the kitchen sink washing up the dishes

from their tea. She turned off the water and looked up at him expectantly. "Is everything okay? What happened?"

He told her briefly, leaving out the scarier details. "I just feel so helpless being so far away."

Ginny studied him, her crooked fingers dripping with sudsy dishwater over the sink. "Do you want some advice from an old woman? An old woman who admittedly has no business telling you what to do?"

"Of course, Ginny. I would treasure your advice."

Her eyes pierced his soul. "Go get her, you fool! Go be with your wife."

T he scent of a wood-burning fire pit drifted in the air and mingled with the sweet cherry blossoms floating overhead. Twenty-four women wedged into lawn chairs and benches occupied the postage-stamp backyard of the book club hostess, but the atmosphere was a little slice of heaven on earth. Most of the women spoke at least some English, and they seemed to hang on Maddie's every word, patiently listening when her hostess thought it necessary to translate a phrase or two.

Maddie thoroughly enjoyed talking about the writing life and how she'd come to be an author. These women had no idea how mundane life on the Kansas prairie could be, or how many hours she spent at her little desk in their basement apartment, or making beds and cleaning toilets at the inn. She hadn't intentionally romanticized her life—that was one of the many things she didn't like about social media—and yet, no matter how many of the less glamorous aspects of her work she shared, most readers did tend to romanticize the life of a writer.

She launched into a horror story about the editing of her first novel. Her editor for that book had been a new college grad who'd practically rewritten every other word of her novel, as if she had to prove her worth to her higher-ups. As she expressed her frustrations as a new writer, the lawn erupted in laughter.

For a minute, Maddie was afraid she'd said something embarrassingly wrong. Her hostess, Veronique, must have sensed her confusion for she turned to Maddie and said in perfect English, "You are delighting the ladies, Madeleine. Please, continue."

Relieved, Maddie picked up where she'd left off. "I was so scared to go to my acquisitions editor and tell her what was happening, but when I finally did, she was aghast. Thankfully, we both had copies of my original manuscript and they kindly assigned me to a new editor. That editor was Janice Hudson—who had written me the kindest, most encouraging rejection letter early in my career. Janice has been my editor on every book since. I truly don't know how I could keep going without her."

A cool breeze fluttered the cherry blossoms, dusting the grass with pollen, and releasing their scent into the late afternoon air. Maddie wished the rest of her events could be as low-key and charming as this one had been. She answered a few more questions, and the hostess transitioned into the book discussion.

It was always fascinating to hear readers' impressions of various scenes from her novels. Every reader brought their own life experiences and sensibilities to the reading, and Maddie always prayed that God would touch each person who read her words with exactly what they needed at that moment in their life.

The afternoon passed quickly and pleasantly with delicious cakes and chocolate, and everyone wanting to practice their English speaking with Maddie and having their photos taken together. She would have plenty of fun pictures to post online tonight.

By the time the last woman said her goodbyes, Maddie was weary, but also thankful several hours of daylight remained. She'd walked past a quaint thrift shop—or friperie, as it was called in French—several times and had been looking for a chance to go in and browse.

She'd changed into her spare walking shoes—that were now

her *only* walking shoes—before leaving Veronique's home, and having gotten her second wind, she entered the friperie with anticipation, inhaling the pleasantly musty scent of old books and ancient pine.

"Bonjour." She greeted the woman behind the checkout desk.

The shopkeeper greeted her likewise, pointed to a stack of shopping baskets that appeared to be antiques themselves, then returned to the book she was reading.

Maddie took the top basket and looped it over one arm, her pulse quickening at the sight of so many wonderful vintage and antique finds. As she wandered through the rabbit warren of rooms, booth after booth of treasures revealed themselves, each with a history she could only guess at. She couldn't buy anything too big unless she had it shipped home, but browsing was half the fun.

She happened across some rustic old keys that would be perfect in a little bowl on her writing desk back home. Keys to the hearts of her characters or keys to the secrets they were hiding. She'd often been inspired by small objects that became symbols for a theme of her story. Or even made their way into the story.

An idea struck, and she went back to the booth where the keys were and chose a few more, dropping them into her basket. They would make lovely giveaways, maybe tied to a pretty ribbon, with a copy of her book once it released.

She thought to snap a few photos of the shop's interior, then took a quick selfie with the shop in the background behind her. But she quickly deleted that after zooming in on her face to reveal the dark circles under her eyes. *Ugh.* She needed to drink more water and get to bed earlier tonight. Jet lag was real.

She reached the back of the shop and started around toward the front on the other side of the building. An artfully displayed booth with a cheery red and cream theme captured her attention. As her eyes roved the shelves and tables, her gaze landed on an oddly familiar sight.

A Franciscan Apple teapot sat proudly on a little glass cake stand. It took her a minute to realize that the glazed, hand-painted earthenware pot was nearly identical to the one she'd knocked off the counter that day in the kitchen of Annabeth's Inn. Annie's teapot. She stared, mouth agape.

Tentatively, she picked it up and waited for it to stir hurtful reminders. But instead, looking at it, holding it, filled her with warm memories of the inn, of the home she shared with Art on the Kansas prairie. A wave of homesickness swept through her, but in a way that only made her grateful for all she had—and eager to return to it. She checked the small tag hanging from the teapot's handle. Thirty-eight euro. Very affordable. And now that she was minus a pair of bulky walking shoes and a few other items, she would have room to carry the teapot back in her luggage.

She peeled the tape off the lid and looked inside to be sure there were no cracks or crazing. How unusual that this little American-made pot had made its way to France. She wished she knew its story. If she hadn't seen with her own eyes the jagged pieces lying on the tile kitchen floor back in Kansas, she would have sworn this *was* Annie's teapot.

She hugged it to herself, remembering Art's anger when he realized the teapot had broken. She still felt bad about it, even though it had been an accident. The teapot was something that had always made their kitchen feel like home. For Art, but for her too. How special it would be to replace it. A way to honor Annie. To show Art that she understood what it meant to him. Because despite the feelings of jealousy she sometimes entertained, Annie had done nothing wrong. In fact, Annie had loved her writing. The notes Annie had left in the margins of Maddie's novels had ultimately brought her and Art together.

The shopkeeper wandered from the front of the store and gave her a questioning look. "Avez-vous trouvé tout ce que vous cherchiez?"

Had she found everything she was looking for? Maddie smiled. "Oui. Yes. Yes, I have. Merci."

The sun was setting quickly and Art pressed the accelerator, wanting to beat the darkness. It had taken several acts of God over the last few days, but plans had fallen into place, and he knew he was doing the right thing.

But there were a few things he still needed to take care of. Things he dreaded even as he knew they were necessary. It struck him that the first was rather like his baptism—an outward symbol of something that had already taken place in his heart.

The Clayburn Cemetery entrance appeared at the top of the hill and he slowed the truck. He turned in and drove over the culvert beneath the high arch of the iron gates, looking beyond the tall posts to the grounds of the cemetery.

He'd never been one for cemeteries and hadn't been here since the Memorial Day after she died when he came to check on her stone. He hoped he could find the spot now. The gravestones suddenly all looked alike.

But then he spotted a familiar copse of trees and a taller stone that he remembered from that Memorial Day because he'd chided himself for following Annie's wishes for a small, flat, unobtrusive stone. She deserved so much more. He parked his truck at the side of the lane and climbed out, walking across the greening grass, dodging other stones as he zigzagged toward her grave.

Then, there it was. It still sometimes took his breath away to realize she was gone. All that remained on this side of the veil was this stone and a myriad of memories.

*Annabeth McGee Tyler*
*Beloved Wife and Daughter*
*April 3, 1982 — April 16, 2019*

He knew Annie wasn't here. But he had some things he needed to say. He took off the tweed cap he wore, clasped it in his hands, and bowed his head over her grave.

"God… Father… I'm here to tell Annie goodbye. I know I said it before, but I'm not sure I understood exactly what that meant then. I do now." He shuffled his feet and smiled. "I know you've been waiting patiently for me to get this over with. I won't pretend to understand how you work these things out, Lord, but I do know that you are good and that what happened to us…you allowed. And now you've graciously allowed Maddie into my life. Ginny says it could even be argued that Annie had a hand in bringing Maddie into my life. I know Annie loved her without ever meeting her. But now I love her too. So…with your help, God, I'm going to give the rest of my life, whatever time you might allow me on this earth, to being the best husband I can be to her. And enjoying every single minute for however long we have. Well, except for cleaning toilets. I reserve the right to despise that the rest of my days."

He could almost hear Annie's laughter. But tears came as he knelt in front of her stone. He didn't believe in talking to the dead. So he trusted that perhaps God would lift the veil of heaven ever so slightly and let his words be heard, for his own sake, more than hers. "You were a gift from God to me, Annie McGee Tyler. And you enriched my life in ways you'll likely never know." He paused, then briefly looked heavenward. "Well, maybe you do know by now. I have missed you so much and I will always carry you with me. So until we meet again, goodbye, Annie…my first love."

He rose to his feet and put his cap back on, and the tightness in his chest began to loosen ever so slightly.

*Thirteen*

Returning to the hotel from a second visit to the Notre-Dame-de-Consolation chapel, Maddie unlocked the door to Room 104 and slipped inside, exhausted.

This tiny hotel room had become a haven to her over the past two weeks of book signings and book club appearances, and—when she could fit them in—research jaunts to the city's libraries and museums. She'd even managed to write the two opening chapters of the first novel in her new series. A rough first draft anyway. And though she was never sure until a book was published and the reviews came in, she thought they were good chapters.

She slipped out of her jacket and shoes and flopped onto the bed. She didn't want to fall asleep so close to bedtime, but after nearly two full weeks here, she still felt jet-lagged. Of course, it didn't help that she was eating more sugar than usual. But who could resist the little macaron cookies that were available at every corner patisserie? Chocolate seemed to be the gift of choice from bookshop owners—and she'd certainly eaten her share. After all, she had scant room to spare in her luggage, and she would not trust le chocolat with La Poste.

Her gaze settled on the teapot atop the secretary desk. That little pot was definitely something she wouldn't trust to any postal service. She would carry it on the plane with her. The hand-painted apple teapot, a twin to Annabeth's, had lived here since the day she'd found it at the friperie. She'd even bought some fragrant loose tea leaves at a charming shop on the Champs-Élysées and had started making her morning tea in the pot, heating water in an electric kettle the hotel provided.

Somehow, looking at the little teapot filled her with a sense of hope. And of home. A connection to the place where her heart belonged, the place she longed to return to. And the man she missed like crazy.

She frowned. How she wished she could change the way she'd left for this trip. Waiting until the very last minute at the airport to tell him she loved him. If only she could go back and do things differently.

She knew Art had forgiven her. But oh, to be able to wipe the slate clean and not have her childish behavior be part of either of their memories. If her immaturity had accomplished anything, it was that she was determined to go home and spend the rest of their lives making new memories. Giving Art memories of a wife who wasn't easily offended, who forgave quickly and completely, who had empathy and sympathy for others instead of being self-centered and easily provoked.

She looked over at the desk, littered with small gifts the book-shop owners had given her as a thank-you for coming. She needed to box them up for mailing home. She thought her book events had gone well and her talks had been well received. Janice had e-mailed to say she was hearing rave reviews. Most of the bookshops had been filled to overflowing for her events, but that wasn't saying much since most of the tiny shops hit maximum capacity at about twenty people. She smiled, imagining Art's laughter when she told him that. Thinking of him made her ache with longing.

One more week and she would be home. Though it seemed

like she'd been gone forever, and one more week felt like an eternity.

Still, she didn't want to waste the gift God had granted in allowing her to be here in Paris. The city was in full bloom now, and it was a delight to wander through the streets in a cloud of pink and coral, to see salmon-colored petals floating on the breeze and dotting the green-brown waters of the Seine. Even so, it all seemed wasted without Art to share it with.

And she couldn't deny that her experience with the thieves who'd stolen her backpack had made her cautious about where she explored and diligent about getting back to the hotel before dark if she couldn't catch a cab.

She closed her eyes, fighting sleep. Why was it taking her so long to get over this jet lag? Of course, it was getting close to that time of the month and she often felt sluggish and out of sorts then. She'd feel better in a few days. Maybe she just needed to eat something—something healthy, since she'd practically eaten her weight in chocolat. But nothing really appealed to her.

She sat up abruptly before she could fall asleep. She slipped on her shoes and went down to the lobby to see if there was anything still on the snack bar.

The small breakfast room was empty but two couples sat together in an alcove just outside the breakfast room having an animated conversation in what she thought was Dutch.

A couple of stale-looking croissants sat under a large glass cloche, but the mini fridge was empty, and now she was starving. It wouldn't be dark for a couple of hours. She could run upstairs and change into comfy shoes and go grab a sandwich at a bistro she'd discovered a couple of blocks away. She hurried past the Dutch couples and started back up the stairs.

Halfway up, a voice stopped her in her tracks. A familiar voice.

She couldn't make out what he was saying, but she *knew* that voice. *Art?* Confused, she reached into her pocket to check her phone thinking maybe he was calling her. But the only thing in her pocket was her room key and a few euros. She'd left her phone in her room.

She went farther up the stairs so she'd be out of sight of the couples in the alcove. But she stopped again around the curve of the steps and held onto the railing, listening.

The deep, warm voice came again—from the lobby! His voice mingled with several others, including Monsieur Bajwa's, but there was no mistaking it.

"Art?" She shouted his name, racing down the stairs, ignoring the couples' stares.

In the lobby, she stopped short. Two women waited in line at the registration desk in deep conversation with Monsieur Bajwa, but the lobby was otherwise empty.

But she was certain she'd heard Art's voice.

She spun and looked back through the alcoves toward the breakfast room. The two couples had resumed their conversation.

She went back and searched the alcoves and the breakfast room, then checked the lobby again. One of the women now stood waiting for the elevator—with a pile of luggage Maddie was quite sure would not fit on the tiny lift. The younger woman was arguing with Monsieur Bajwa—something about their keys. Maddie listened again for Art's voice.

Nothing. She must have been imagining things. Even so, disappointment almost brought her to tears. She missed him desperately. And right now, she couldn't bear to go back up to her room and be alone another night.

Her stomach growled, reminding her of the mission she'd been on. She looked down at the slip-on shoes she wore. No farther than she had to go to the bistro, they would be fine. She was famished.

She felt in her pocket for her key. She wouldn't be gone long and didn't want to wait at the desk to turn it in.

She exited through the sliding doors and headed around the back of the hotel toward Rue Bertin Poirée, avoiding the alley where she'd been attacked. But she felt disconcerted. She could have sworn she'd heard Art's voice in the lobby. Maybe it was just an American voice that stood out amidst all the foreign accents and her mind had turned it into Art's voice. Was she so homesick that she was hallucinating?

Art checked the room number again and mindful of the other doors in the hallway, knocked softly. "Maddie? Hey, it's me."

He waited but no answer and he couldn't hear any sounds on the other side of the door. The concierge had informed him "Madame Houser" had likely not left the hotel since her key was not at the desk. Surely Maddie would have told him if she'd changed hotels. He'd encouraged her to do that after the attack, but she'd insisted she was safe here. And now that he was here, it did seem to be a safe part of the city and a well-run hotel. The man at the desk—the same one he'd had the long-distance phone conversation with judging by his accent—wouldn't give him any information at all about Maddie until he showed his ID and revealed that he already knew her room number. The man had offered to ring Maddie's room to let her know he'd arrived, but Art was still hoping the element of surprise would work in his favor.

He knocked once more to no avail. Now what? He hadn't called Maddie, wanting to surprise her, but now doubts slipped in. What if she didn't consider him showing up in the middle of her book tour a happy surprise? Their conversations—brief as they'd been—had been increasingly warmer, but what if she still needed time to work things through?

But he was here now. He wasn't about to fly home without seeing her. Neither did he want to hang out in the hotel lobby until she returned from wherever she was. And he felt certain the concierge would not let him into Maddie's room. At least he hoped the hotel had better security policies than that.

He dialed her cell phone and waited. A familiar ringtone came from behind the door to Room 104. What? She was here? She must be sleeping.

He knocked louder. "Maddie, wake up! It's me." He risked a glance down the short hallway, expecting doors to open and angry guests to stick their heads out and shush him. Sound carried through the thin walls of these old hotels.

He tried calling again, heard the ringing from behind the door, but waited for voicemail this time and left a message. "Hey, Maddie. Call me when you get this, please." Remembering the time difference, given that she thought he was in Kansas, he added, "No matter what time it is."

He hung up before realizing that his message would no doubt make her think something awful had happened in Kansas.

Maybe he could have the front desk call her. She might respond to the phone by her bedside ringing. Why was she sleeping at five in the afternoon though? He didn't like this one bit.

Fourteen

Walking back to the hotel, Maddie ate the savory falafel on pita bread, not caring if she dripped tahini sauce on her clothes. The sandwich was delicious and getting something in her stomach made her feel somewhat better, though she could still hear Art's voice in her head the way it had sounded at the hotel. As real as if he'd been in the next room. He would no doubt get a kick out of the story when she told him about it. Especially since it could only be interpreted one way: she missed him like crazy.

She counted down the days until she could go home. Paris was indescribably lovely, she was here at the absolutely perfect time of year, and it had been an incredibly worthwhile trip as far as her career and the research for her novels was concerned.

But she was homesick. She missed her husband desperately. And she cherished that fact, given the less-than-ideal terms they'd parted on. But no one had told her that homesickness was a literal, bodily illness. Whenever she thought of Art and the fathomless miles that separated them, she felt a little nauseous. At least she knew the remedy for what ailed her. And by this time next week, she would be in the grip of that handsome "cure."

The dark red awning of the hotel appeared as she rounded the corner and she sighed, dreading the empty room that awaited her. She was thankful she had her key with her and wouldn't need to stop at the front desk for it since she was a rather bedraggled mess with her hair falling out of the neat updo she'd started with this morning, all her makeup worn off, and now, spots of tahini sauce decorating her wrinkled shirt.

She waited for the second set of sliding doors to open, then walked with purpose toward the stairway, weary and wanting to avoid the customary greetings from the Bajwas.

Halfway up the stairs, Madame Bajwa called her name.

With a sigh, she returned to the lobby.

"Ah, there you are, Madame. You have someone who—"

"Hi Maddie." Art stood with his back to the registration desk, his stance assured and authoritative.

Maddie took a few steps toward the desk, praying she wasn't now seeing things as well as hearing Art's voice. But no, it was him. He was here! She couldn't seem to find her voice.

He opened his arms and she ran into his embrace, squishing what was left of her supper between them.

After a long minute soaking up his warmth, she leaned away and studied his face, trying to convince herself she wasn't imagining things. But he was as real as the squashed sandwich in her hand. The tears came then, and she couldn't seem to stop them. "I can't believe you're really here. Oh, honey, I must look like a mess! But what on earth are you doing here?"

A glint came to his eyes. "I can go back if you don't want me here."

She pulled him to her again. "Don't you dare. Oh, Art! I can't believe it. You're really here!"

He kissed her quickly, then pulled her to one side of the desk, turning back to Madame Bajwa. "Thank you, Madame. I found what I was looking for."

"Oui, indeed, you did." Grinning broadly, she gave Maddie a knowing look.

Maddie brushed the tears from her cheeks and turned her smile on Madame Bajwa. She probably should introduce Art to the couple who'd rescued her the night she was attacked, but right now, she just wanted to lead him up to her room, kiss his handsome face, and give him a proper welcome. But also to hear what wonders had brought him across the ocean to her.

Suddenly it struck her that something might have happened at home. "Is...is everything okay?" she whispered.

He pulled her closer. "It is now."

She looked down at his suitcase with his long winter coat lopped over the handle. "You're not going to need that."

"It was cold in Kansas when I left."

"Well, it's spring here. Come on. Let's get you settled. You must be exhausted."

He glanced toward the tiny elevator.

She laughed. "You might prefer to take the stairs. Unless you want to go by yourself. It's kind of a one-man lift."

"Stairs it is. But I'm getting tired of lugging this suitcase up these stairs."

She gave him a questioning look.

"I'll explain later." He laughed and followed her to the broad carpeted staircase.

At the top, breathless, she turned to him. "Oh Art... I can't believe you're really here."

He pulled her close for another kiss. "Let me in so I can put down this luggage and kiss you properly."

This time she had no problem fitting the key in the lock.

Art took in the cozy room with its stone walls and lace curtains fluttering in the evening breeze. He set his suitcase down by the wall adjacent to the door, lopped his jacket over the luggage, and turned to pull Maddie into his arms.

A low groan escaped him. "Madeleine Houser, do you have any idea how much I've missed you?"

She cradled his face in her hands and looked up at him. "It's Tyler, in case you forgot. Madeleine *Tyler*, and you couldn't have missed me any more than I've missed you."

"Wanna bet?"

"Let's not argue."

He pulled her even closer, desire rising in him. How he'd missed this woman. "I love you, Maddie. So very much."

"And I love you. So very much."

It seemed to him that they were both trying, with their words, to atone for the unfinished argument that had preceded her trip to Paris. But he didn't want to take anything for granted. "Can you forgive me?"

"Oh, Art. It's me who needs to ask forgiveness."

"Let's meet halfway, shall we?"

She laughed softly. "You're the one who came five thousand miles."

He wove his fingers through her hair and gathered her to his chest. "And I'm so glad I did."

"But why?"

"Why did I come?" He sat on the low bed and pulled her down beside him. "The truth?"

She nodded.

"Ginny made me." He laughed "No, that's not quite right. But she gave me permission."

"I don't understand."

He told her about his conversation with Ginny. "When I heard what happened—that you were attacked—oh, Maddie, I can't even tell you how helpless I felt."

"I'm fine."

"You're sure?" In truth, she looked thinner and a little pale. But maybe it was just the dim evening light.

"I'm fine, honey. Truly."

"I'm glad then. And Maddie—" He was too wiped out from

the flight to be having this conversation now. He didn't want to mess up and say the wrong thing again. But he continued anyway. "I should have come with you in the first place."

She nodded. "And I should have waited until you could."

Her words were a balm, as he hoped his had been for her. He looked around the tiny room that had been home to Maddie for these two weeks. A whole world that he wasn't part of. He felt jealous of Paris. His gaze wandered to a small secretary-type desk against the brick wall. And there on top— "Maddie? What's this?"

She followed his line of sight to the teapot perched on the desk. Annie's teapot. "I found it at a friperie—a thrift shop—here. Can you believe it? I know it's not Annie's and I realize hers can never be replaced, but maybe this one can remind us of hers? Are you okay with that? We don't have to keep it if it...bothers you," she added quickly.

"No. I...I can't believe you found one like it. Exactly like it." He rose and went to lift the teapot. It felt different than Annie's. Why, he wasn't sure. Still, it felt like finding something precious that he'd lost. "It means the world that you bought it, Maddie. Truly. Thank you."

He laid back on the bed, exhaustion overcoming him. Maddie scooted beside him and he pulled her close. She curled up with her head on his chest, one hand cupping his stubbly cheek. It felt so utterly right to have her in his arms again.

But he didn't want to smooth things over too quickly just because they were together. "We'll talk it all through, okay? Everything. I want to be sure you feel heard. That you know how sorry I am. And I don't want to rush you or skate over anything just for the sake of having peace between us." He yawned. "But right now, love, I'm so weary I'm afraid anything I said would only make matters worse."

She patted his cheek and sighed, snuggling closer. "I love you, Art. All that matters is that you're here now. If you'd told me this morning that I would be falling asleep in your arms by nightfall, I wouldn't have believed it. But I'm so glad. So very glad."

She echoed his yawn and snuggled closer. "I'm tired too."

He lay there feeling her heart beat against his side, relishing the softness of her skin beneath his fingers. And the last sound he heard before he drifted off was the soothing music of her quiet, even breaths against his chest.

Morning's first rays of sun filtered through the curtains creating ripples of dappled light on the white bedsheets. Maddie slowly opened her eyes and smiled when she realized her husband's handsome head was on the pillow beside her. The joy of last night's surprise hit her all over again. He'd come all the way to Paris to be with her. It still seemed surreal.

She couldn't cancel her remaining book events, but she and Art could steal a few hours each day to explore the city and just be together. And he would be here in this room, in this bed beside her each evening as they found their way back to each other.

He stirred beside her and reached for her.

"Good morning," she whispered in his ear.

"Mmm... Good morning, love. Would you mind too much if we just stayed in bed all day?"

She laughed and scooted closer. "My book signing isn't until two o'clock. Exactly what did you have in mind?"

The next days with Art in Paris felt like a romantic scene from one of her favorite novels. He came with her to a couple of her book signings and was so sweetly complimentary it almost embarrassed her. She suspected he was trying to make up for what had happened at the now-infamous faculty gathering, but she knew him well enough to believe his praise was sincere. And she treasured it.

When she wasn't signing books or meeting with book clubs, they walked all over the city and reveled in the springtime blooms. "Not that I didn't love our St. Louis honeymoon," he told her one day when they walked under cherry blossoms with the Eiffel Tower as a backdrop, "but this is the honeymoon I really wanted to give you."

"Well, I loved St. Louis with you, too, but I love the price tag on this one. And that we're not paying it!"

"I didn't tell you how much those last-minute flights of mine cost, did I?"

She put a finger over his mouth. "Shhh, let's not spoil it, okay? It's still cheaper than if we were paying for everything ourselves."

"Maybe. Slightly." But his smile said he was teasing.

This morning she'd taken him to Notre-Dame-de-Consolation where the contemporary storylines of her first novel would be set. She'd wanted Art to be able to picture everything she'd been talking about, but it also gave her a chance to check on some details she'd forgotten when she'd been there before.

They'd declared it a "Chapel Day" and from there, they'd gone to the "real" Notre Dame, though they weren't able to go inside, since the gorgeous cathedral was still under construction after the fire that had done such horrific damage a few years ago. Writing about these tragic conflagrations had certainly given her a deep respect for the power of fire. And the lives that were changed because of its wrath.

Now they were walking the short distance to Sainte-Chapelle, a majestic chapel constructed in the early 1200s and that had been the residence of the kings of France until the 14th century. It was hard to fathom the age of most everything in Paris. It made one feel rather small. She'd been here eight years ago and it had been high on her list of things to see again, but she hadn't gotten around to it until now.

Art tousled her hair. "You're awfully quiet. What's going on in that pretty head of yours?"

She smiled up at him. "I'm just glad you're here with me."

"Good answer. But is that all?"

"I'm thinking about my books. And what a wonderful thing it's been to be able to come and do this research. I honestly don't know if I could have done the stories justice without this trip."

"I understand that after seeing the site of the fire. I'm sorry I was reluctant to let you go."

"No, don't be, Art. I understand why you were. And I consider it a compliment. I'm sorry I used it as an excuse to run away."

The floodgates opened then, and as they walked in one of the prettiest places on Planet Earth, all the hurts and tears and sorrow were laid on the table, examined, and then allowed to fall away under the power of forgiveness—God's forgiveness and their willingness to extend forgiveness to each other.

An hour later, after a simple lunch at a charming bistro, it was their turn to step inside Sainte-Chapelle and climb the winding stone steps to the stunning stained-glass chapel. They looked up, speechless, as a myriad of colors danced in the light, bathing the entire room in all the shades of the rainbow. Standing behind Maddie, Art wrapped his arms around her and she leaned her head against his shoulder, staring up at the most glorious work of art she'd ever seen.

The panels that created an entire ceiling of stained glass told God's story from Genesis to Revelation. From His creation to His ultimate sacrifice.

Standing in the arms of the husband God had blessed her with, Maddie didn't think it was lost on either of them what an infinitesimal part of His creation they were. And yet, somehow, He knew them and loved them and cared that they made things right between them. It was too much to take in.

Walking back to the hotel, holding hands, they talked quietly. As they shared their hearts, shared their awe in all God had done in their lives, she could almost feel the healing that was being completed inside each of them. She looked up at him, still astonished that he was here. "Oh, Art... I think we both were clinging so hard to what we thought was most dear to us, we couldn't see that what's actually most dear to us is *us.*"

"You do have a way with words, love." Art winked and planted a kiss on her cheek. "Have you ever considered being a writer?"

*Fifteen*

"I kind of like this extended spring we're having. Spring in Paris and now spring in Kansas." Art bent over the steering wheel and looked out over the Kansas prairie, eager to get home after the long flight.

Maddie followed his gaze through the windshield as they turned onto Hampton Road. Their road. Blooming crab apples and redbuds dotted the landscape, and a haze of green colored the tree branches in the pastures and farmyards. "Let's do it every year, shall we?"

He laughed. "If you hit the *New York Times* bestseller list, we will."

"Oh, I doubt I'll ever be that"—she tossed him a smirk and circled for the landing—"*popular*."

His face bloomed into a huge grin. "Oooh, touché. Nicely done, Madame Houser."

She laughed. It felt good to finally be able to joke about what had once been so hurtful. "Oh, honey, it's so good to be home." She meant so much more than home to the inn.

And the knowing look he gave her said he understood. "We're almost there. And it is good."

"It feels like I've been gone for a lifetime."

"That's how it felt to me without you here. A lifetime."

She reached over and put a hand on his knee. "Thank you for making the trip. I can't say it enough, Art. I—" The lump in her throat wouldn't let her say more.

Within minutes a familiar rooftop came into sight. Art pulled into the driveway slowly.

The house looked beautiful, just as she'd seen it in her dreams all those homesick nights in Paris. But something was different. The fruit trees in the yard were in full bloom, but there was something else.

The sign. The *Annabeth's Inn* sign was gone. "Art? What happened? Did we have a storm while I was gone? The sign..."

He shook his head but kept his eyes on the driveway. "I took it down. Before I left for Paris."

"What? Why?"

"It just seemed like it was time."

"But... Does that mean you are—*we* are closing the inn?"

"Not until you're ready. But GPS gets people here just fine. And we'll want the sign gone when this is just a house—*our* house."

"Our *home*," she whispered.

"We still have bookings about nine months out, but we can close our reservation calendar whenever you think we should."

"I think we should."

"Really?" He put the truck in Park and unbuckled his seatbelt. "You're ready to close the inn?"

"You wouldn't mind?"

"Not at all. You know I've been ready for a while."

"Well, ready or not, I think it's time." Her heart beat a quick staccato.

"You sound pretty sure."

"I am sure." She smiled up at him. "And nine months sounds just about right."

He stared. "What do you mean?"

She spread her hand across her belly where she'd begun to

suspect a new life grew. "I'm late. Two weeks late, in fact. And I think I know why I've been so exhausted recently."

Understanding came to his eyes. "Are you serious? Maddie, are you serious?"

She couldn't help the broad smile that came. "I'm pretty stinkin' serious. You're...okay with that?"

"I could not possibly be more okay with that. Oh, Maddie..." He leaned across the console and gathered her into his arms. "This is the best news ever, love! But... When will you know for sure?"

She smiled and melted into the warmth of his embrace, breathing in the lingering scent of his aftershave. "I'll buy an at-home test when we get groceries. But I'm pretty certain what it will say."

An hour later, with their suitcases unpacked, the washing machine and dryer running, and Alex purring in her arms, Maddie followed Art through the house planning and dreaming.

He stopped in the doorway of the main floor bedroom. "We could turn this into a playroom, don't you think?"

"It would be perfect." She could just picture a little play kitchen in the corner by the window. And one of those carpets that had little two-lane roads printed on it for driving Matchbox cars on. "And maybe we could get my piano out of storage and move it in here? Make this into a music room too?"

He nodded. "It would be wonderful to have music in the house again."

"Um..." She feigned a grimace and deposited Alex on the floor. "You haven't heard me play yet. I play by heart, remember? You might not consider it music. And a toddler banging on the piano is just noise."

He lopped his arm around her shoulders, leaned against the door jamb, and pulled her close. "It will all be music to me, love. The very best kind of music."

DEBORAH RANEY's first novel, *A Vow to Cherish*, inspired the World Wide Pictures film of the same title and launched Deb's writing career. Forty books later, she's still creating stories that touch hearts and lives. A RITA Award, Carol Award, and National Readers Choice Award winner and three-time Christy Award finalist, Deb is a recent transplant to Missouri, having moved with her husband, Ken Raney, from their native Kansas. They love road trips, Friday garage sale dates, time with their kids and grandkids, and breakfast on the screened porch overlooking their wooded backyard.

Visit Deb on the Web at www.deborahraney.com.

For other books
by Deborah Raney

To learn more, visit:
deborahraney.com